This book is for you if.....

...you love Science Fiction

...you have a love for action & adventure stories

...you like Aeroplanes

...you like Technology and Engineering

...you like hearing about Family interaction

...you ever wondered how it might be after WW3

...you like CGI (Computer Generated Imagery)

...you like stereoscopic 3D

...you like Music in the Rock and Pop genre

...you believe you should never give up

...you are looking for a Fun read

...you like diverse characters

What people are saying

Reviewer 1:
This is not just a reading book – it's a whole multimedia experience.

Reviewer 2: Obido Samuel Chiemerie from Online Book Club says...

Jack Ezra's "The Family Flyer and the Boomerang Beast" brilliantly merges storytelling with multimedia elements, creating a richly immersive experience. With its engaging narrative, innovative use of CGI, and an accompanying music album, Ezra's work transcends traditional books, offering a unique and captivating read. This inventive blend of text, visuals, and sound makes it a standout in modern literature, earning a well-deserved 5-star rating.

Reviewer 3: Bakka Bhai from OnlineBookClub says...

Jack Ezra, a very talented person skilled in design, writing, drawing, inventing, and music, has created a new book called "The Family Flyer and the Boomerang Beast."

Set in a troubled future, the book tells the story of a strong family - Kat, Jack, and Skye - searching for their missing teenage son after a terrible global war.

They live in an old nuclear bunker and build a special plane called the Family Flyer.

Their journey leads them to a university where they find other survivors and make new friends, including Banshee, a transgender student and singer who revives the city's radio station.

The story becomes more exciting as they face a scary creature in the university's basement, deal with rival clans, and fight off intruders when they return home.

This book stands out because it uses multimedia elements. It includes over 100 computer-made images, a 15-song music album you can download, and cool 3D visuals.

The Limited Edition A4 paperback even comes with free 3D glasses so readers can enjoy the visuals fully.

These features make the book more engaging and unique compared to traditional books.

Jack Ezra blends imagination with technology, focusing on family, survival, and innovation. The characters are well-developed, each adding their own strengths and weaknesses to the story. The plot is exciting and full of surprises, keeping readers hooked. The use of CGI and music enhances the emotional and visual impact of the story.

"The Family Flyer and the Boomerang Beast" highlights Jack Ezra's creativity and ability to go beyond traditional storytelling. By combining writing, CGI, and music, he has created a book that is not only fun to read but also visually and emotionally captivating. The book is well-crafted, with no errors, and is sure to impress readers.

I'd love to rate this book a solid 5 out of 5 stars. There was nothing that I disliked about this book.

This book is highly recommended for those who enjoy immersive storytelling and want a unique reading experience that combines a rich story with technological innovation.

Jack Ezra recording in a Music Studio.

Story outline...

In the near future the deadly pink mist and the radiation from the world war has harmed the Earth.

For three years Kat, Jack and Skye support each other in their renovated nuclear bunker designing and building their Family Flyer aeroplane so they can search for their missing teenage son.

First stop - the university, where survivors are surprised to see the family and their amazing aircraft.

Banshee, a singer and transgender student befriends the family and reinstates the radio station in the city but first, there is a monster in the basement which needs to be neutralised.

Next stop the Family meet the children of the two warring clans but wait... who is the Boomerang Beast and what is his secret?

How is it possible that the children of the Biter Clan are able to eat fruit which should have killed them?

Can the Family secure peace between the two fighting clans?

All of this is nothing compared to returning home to find intruders who want everything the family own and a tense battle ensues.

The Family enjoying some high action training.

Jack   **Kat**   **Skye**   **3J's**

About the Author

Jack Ezra is a Design Technology teacher, writer, illustrator, inventor and musician, currently with five Music Albums selling in 143 Countries.

He has created several stories and film scripts in the past and directed or produced some of them.

Before teaching DT, he won five Research and Development government grant awards for innovative technology.

His passion for writing, CGI, technology and music have all come together in this unique Family Flyer, project.

Aknowledgements

I would like to thank Tracy and Jet for their love, support and feedback during the two years while creating the music and artwork for this project.

Also, thanks Tracy, for singing on "Simply Just A Man", one of the songs that goes with this book.

I would like to thank Chris Day of Filiment Publishing for his gererous Forward in this book and his guidance and encouragement in finilising the Family Flyer project.

Dedication

We've heard the phrase...
"You can choose your friends but you can't choose your Family" and sadly, I have nodded my head in agreement to this statement too many times during my life.

I have seen and heard how some families treat each other very badly and are unkind and distant from one other, but on the other hand, I have also seen how some families care and risk all for each other.

So I dedicate all my endeviours in the creation of the Family Flyer, in the hope that it all works out well for my family and yours, in the end.

This book is dedicated to Family's all over the world, wishing for peace, togetherness, understanding, happiness and love.

Banshee **Dean Grey** **Mati** **BB**

Enjoy a new Dimention
with the
Limited Edition Version

A BOOK LIKE NO OTHER.

Containing over 100 Computer Generated Images.

15 Song Music Album to download.

3D Images which jump off the page.

FREE 3D Glasses with the Limited Edition Stereoscopic 3D version.

For the latest news or where to purchase 3D glasses, the digital or Limited Edition Stereoscopic 3D version and for all the latest information on all things Family Flyer.

website: https://www.thefamilyflyer.com

THE **FAMILY FLYER** AND THE **BOOMERANG BEAST**

JACK EZRA

Published by
Filament Publishing Ltd
14, Croydon Road, Beddington
Croydon, Surrey CR0 4PA

+44 (0)20 8688 2598
www.filamentpublishing.com

The Family Flier and the Boomerang Beast
by Jack Ezra

© 2025 Jack Ezra

ISBN 978-1-915465-67-2

Printed in the UK.

Table of Contents

Chapter 1:   Before the Flyer.   14

Chapter 2:   Martin the Messenger.   30

Chapter 3:   The Boomerang Beast.   62

Chapter 4:   The Apple Orchard.   78

Chapter 5:   Jimi Jack's Dream.   94

Chapter 6:   The Care Home.   106

Chapter 7:   Back To Freedom Point.   124

Chapter 8:   Jimi Jack's Journey.   128

Chapter 9:   Invaders.   156

Music Album Details.   176

Song Lyrics x 15.   178

Bernie   Nina   Tina   Alien   Monsters

Forward

What? No Klingons?

If you look back at how science fiction writing has evolved over the decades you will find that there are very few completely original writers.

So many have built on the originality of the few and made a name for themselves by being inspired by others ideas. Ever the monsters and the aliens seem to have come from the same genes.

It take more though than just originality to tell a good story and to keep the reader wondering what is coming next. It takes great imagination.

In the exciting new book, "The Family Flier and the Boomerang Beast", Jack Ezra conclusively proves that he has both.

Far from introducing us to a battalion of little green men to stretch our credibility and distract us from the flow of the story, his plot is perfectly believable and could be just around the corner, where we can't yet see.

With so much talk of war and nuclear weapons, who is to say that we won't wake up one day to the consequences of such a conflict.How would we react?

Probably not as well as the characters in this gripping book!

If you are a fan of sci-fi and love a good adventure, then this book is for you!

The author has a great advantage by being a Design Technology teacher, writer, illustrator, inventor and musician, currently, with five Music Albums selling in 148 Countries. For him, life is a daily creativity playground, as the ideas in the book, prove.

I congratulate Jack on both his imagination as well as his execution of a book that is indeed "like none other!"

Chris Day MD Filament Publishing Ltd

CHAPTER 1

Before the Flyer.

The nuclear winter lasted three long years. The bombs caused so much damage, death and destruction to our nearby town and when the dust went up into the atmosphere, it blocked out the sun for over 36 months.

It was now much darker and colder than we were used to and it felt just like a constantly cloudy, winters day.

The other problem was that the pink mist accompanied the cold weather and if you went outside and breathed the air in for any length of time you would certainly become ill and the chances of survival was very low.

The pink mist was the result of the virus released by the Sad Sun terrorists, mixing with the radioactive dust from their dirty bombs.

It looked pink and very pretty sometimes but you would not last very long without your gas mask outside.

The government issued lockdown instructions for what was left of the remaining population to stay inside until further notice and so that is exactly what we did for, what seemed like an eternity but we were far luckier than most people because of where we lived.

Kathleen, my wife, or Kat as I call her, and I, raised our children in the nuclear bunker that Kat and I bought for just a single one-dollar bill.

"One Dollar", people often ask, for a huge underground military base worth several million dollars in its heyday, about eighty years ago.

Yes, and for that very reason it did make the headlines around the world for a couple of weeks. We were featured on TV, in the tabloids and in various magazines, some stating the incredible business opportunity side of it, while some articles focused on our family and how we were going to build this business opportunity from a rundown, cold-war, nuclear bunker and develop it into a modern aircraft museum attraction and even to extend it into a school of engineering with a lecture theatre and accommodation for hundreds of students.

I should explain a little about it if you did not see us on TV or picked up any magazines or tabloid newspapers about it, as yet.

Magazines interested in the story of the Family.

The newly weds

Kat was really the one who earned the big money. She was the international fashion model bringing in millions a year.

You would know her as Hannah Hendrix and if you saw her, you would know that with her looks, she had to be a model or an actress or something like that.

She was beautiful, athletic and the most caring person I have ever met.

So of course, I married her but, I digress, I was going to explain about the one dollar deal we did with the Ministry of Defence.

"Freedom Point", was the name of the secret nuclear bunker situated deep in the limestone mountains. It used to be able to launch Inter Continental Ballistic Missiles or ICBMs from silos within the mountain, now covered over by the pair of helipads on the uppermost level of the base where we built our house and the swimming pool.

I had the crazy idea that we could renovate this huge bunker, make it into some kind of an aircraft museum attraction and even live there.

So, when Kat agreed to put her money in with mine and the Ministry of Defence sold the base to us for a single dollar we were over the moon.

We were then offered a "Times Two" business grant.

The way the grant worked was that whatever you put into an approved and viable business venture, the grant would times the funds you put in, by two.

So, Kat put in two million, I put in a million also, and the grant doubled what we invested giving us 3 million more.

I guess they thought it would be beneficial to the employment of the local town and the economy.

So, within six months we owned a huge military establishment for a single dollar bill but had to put in our own funds of three million which was further added to by the grant.

So, in reality we had actually started a new attraction business venture which was going to cost a few millions and one dollar, to renovate.

I guess the one-dollar deal was a legal requirement to pass over the full and legal ownership of the "Freedom Point" base to us and we used it conveniently to generate press and TV, which it certainty did.

The day of the bombs

Oh, my one million.
I forgot to mention that before I became a technology teacher, I was in the music business.

I had some success writing songs for a number of international artists and even had some chart success of my own with three music albums.

Then, I sold off a couple of inventions and a business idea to a large company and the bank gave me a start-up loan, too.

I mentioned that Kat & I raised our two children, but in reality, I should say we looked after our daughter Skye Jett, because the day the bombs hit, Jimi Jack, our son, was away on a camping field trip with his school for a week but he never returned and we never heard from any living soul after that.

Jimi Jack was sixteen then, so assuming that he is still alive today, he would now be nineteen.

I wish I had the sense to keep him at home that day, because in the weeks leading up to the dirty bomb & virus bomb explosions, I began to sense the world was hitting a crisis point.

Religion had always brought wars throughout history, but the Sad Sun Environmental group joined forces with a religious terrorist group and before too long the occasional suicide bomb, terror attack grew to became regular, chemical virus attacks, which later became dirty bomb nuclear strikes on towns and cities. People died in the hundreds of thousands per day.

Our local city was reduced to nothing more than rubble, with a few brave buildings leaning painfully, away from the direction of the blasts.

The once proud buildings stood, desolate silhouettes against the dark perilous, pink, radioactive, skyline, and the air, now unbreathable, and our beloved country lay bleak and ashen grey in the three-year winter which followed.

Luckily, we had the sense to build our home at the top of Freedom Point, and we filled the hangers and the house with tinned provisions, dry pasta, tankers of water, petrol, jet fuel and equipment.

Enough to last a decade at least. Even the house and pool were protected by a unique movable dome which I could activate in to place over the house, with a single press of a button on my iPad.

Our hideaway home was spacious, safe and comfortable, and yet every day I reassured Kathleen that we would find our boy, Jimi Jack and every so often she would cry a few more tears for our desolated family, our destroyed country and our devastated planet.

The crashed Piper plane

Days in the mountain home-bunker turned into weeks, which turned into months and then into the three long years, until one day we heard a sound that we had not heard in a very long time.

It was a distant whisper at first, becoming louder as each minute stretched my ears and my imagination.

The raspy, spluttering turned into a continuous grunt, which very quickly became the sound of a small aircraft flying overhead, and it seemed like it was in serious trouble.

A few seconds later and we felt, more than we heard, the vibration of an explosion through the solid limestone mountain.

The three of us immediately kitted ourselves out with masks and some fire extinguishers and went on a scouting expedition and fifteen minutes later we confirmed our worst fears.

A family had crashed their small yellow, Piper aeroplane on the other side, and at the base of the mountain, in the main entrance carpark, and it looked like no one had survived. The airplane had disintegrated when it smashed against the thick concrete bunker walls and many of the parts were on fire.

The man in the front seat had blood on his face, and from the obtuse angle of his head I guessed he had broken his neck. The woman, who I assumed was his wife, sat beside him, the half-round steering wheel nowhere to be seen, and only the shaft remaining, where it had pierced her chest all the way through.

The two small children, a boy and a girl, brought tears to my eyes. They looked so beautiful, without a single mark on their face or their bodies, and looked as if they were sleeping. Of course, Kathleen and I both checked their pulses a few times, once we put the fire in the cabin out, but we knew they were dead.

Even if the family had survived the initial impact of the crash they were certainly not suitably equipped with chemical or radiation suits to protect themselves, and probably would have perished within hours of the crash.

Later we buried the family on a green grass patch just on the other side of where they crashed into the thick concrete bunker wall. We placed a sign in memory of the unknown family who died here, and then we salvaged as much of the contents of the aeroplane, and as many of the mechanical parts as we could, and as we headed back up to the house, I had a new plan.

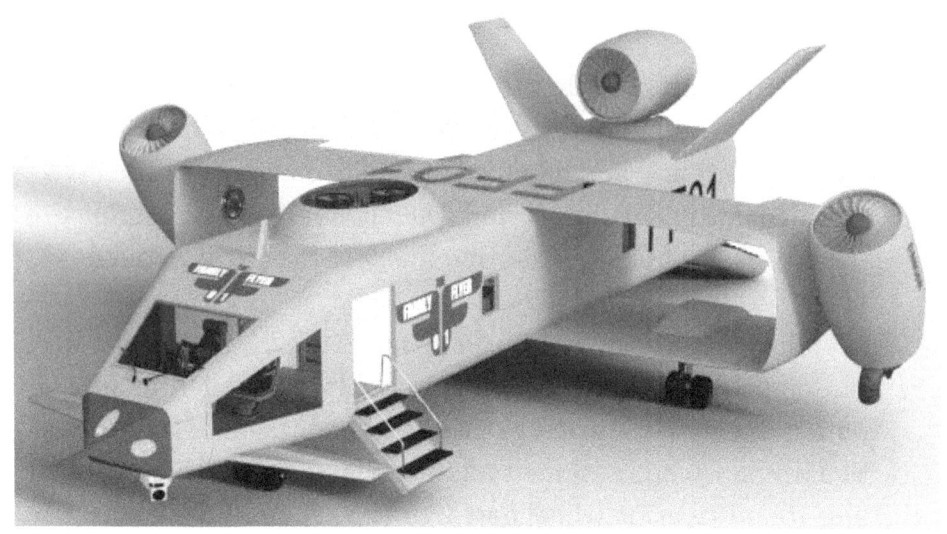

The Family Flyer

For the next few weeks, during the day, I equipped one of the hangers with an overhead crane and welding equipment, while Kat continued home-schooling Skye using the computer equipment I had carefully decontaminated from the nearby town and restored.

Then in the evenings the three of us set about designing and building our very own flying machine.

The design was partly based on the Lockheed Martin HC130 or the Hercules as most people knew them, only, our aeroplane was going to have a square cabin, large cockpit windows and a different ramp tail door, and in contrast to the 130, it was going to be a vertical take-off and landing biplane, as I had a few ducted fan jet engines I wanted to use and thought a biplane would have more lift and take up less wing span.

I thought of a couple of other novel modifications I could add too.

We would be able to pilot it like an airplane simulator game via Wi-Fi from any iPad or our phones or even use inexpensive gaming joysticks.

The two fan jet engines would swivel downwards and also backwards, so we could take off and land vertically, and yet point them backwards in flight to push the airplane forwards with a third jet engine at the back which could also swivel left, right or face forwards if ever the need arose to fly backwards.

I would make the aeroplane as comfortable as our mountain home duplicating our main bedroom and have another bedroom for Skye & Jimi to share.

There would be two toilets and a shower room, a living room, a kitchen with dining table and even a big TV screen.

I would store fuel and water, the batteries, camping equipment, bedding, cooking utensils, tools and basically, anything else I thought we might need, in storage cupboards all around the airplane.

It took the three of us almost all of the thirty-six months of the lockdown period, designing, building and testing our new airplane, and all the time the outdoor sensors showed that chemical and radioactive readings were nearly low enough to venture outside without our masks and safe suits.

Of course, we would never do anything like that because there would always be pockets of higher radioactive and chemical readings in some places and they could be fatal to anyone without protective equipment.

The Family putting the Entrance sign up.

We also missed Jimi Jack every day and mentioned him all the time we did anything, wondering where he was and what he was doing or if he was missing us as much as we missed him.

I would glance at Kat anytime Jimi Jack's name was mentioned and sensed her pain as tears welled up and she looked down doing her best, trying not to cry.

Before the day the bombs hit, we spent six months all working together as a family at Freedom Point, putting up signs, clearing rocks, painting and decorating before the day Jimi Jack went missing, and that was almost three years ago.

Once I was happy with the seating, lighting and the control software of our new aeroplane, I practiced hovering in the big white hanger.

First on tethers attached to the wheels, the nose and the tail, then I programmed the proximity sensors to keep the airplane stable on vertical take-off and landing by sending reflected infra-red signals to the ground, and all around, and bouncing them back to the aeroplane.

Then we flew ten feet in the air without lines, Skye in the front pilot's seat and Kat in the seat next to her.

The airplane was so easy to manoeuvre that I even let Skye pilot it on her own after a few practices.

She became quite an expert at take-off and landing, and gentle rotations in the confines of the large white hanger.

We even practiced flying the airplane with our iPads and our iPhones like it was some kind of remote controlled toy.

We did this many times over several weeks until the day came when readings outside looked almost normal.

I slid our home protective dome open and the three of us made our way to the white hanger on the third level where our new aeroplane awaited us.

I slid the giant hanger doors open and stepped out into the warm sun.

At first it dazzled me.

I had not seen such a blue sky and such bright sunlight for such a long time and we had all forgotten what warm sunlight felt like on our faces.

Bringing the Family Flyer out for the first time.

I beckoned to Skye to power up the airplane and fly slowly behind me as I walked forward.

Kat walked alongside the Flyer, one hand gently holding on to the corner of the doorway stairs as her daughter controlled the aeroplane.

This lasted a few moments until Skye brought the airplane down even lower almost touching the tarmac.

Skye disembarked, stepping down gingerly and holding on to the iPad which was controlling the airplane.

She said, "It's OK, Dad, I have her under control".

The engines purred like a happy kittens as the aeroplane hovered inches off the ground.

Then it was my turn, so I climbed abord and closed the door, settled into the pilot's seat and smiled to the girls, waving outside the windows. I gestured for them to step back as I strapped on the seat belt.

I set the altitude to one thousand feet and touched "Go" on the iPad, and the craft shot straight upwards into the bright blue sky, and after a few moments, it hovered there at an altitude of exactly one thousand feet.

I could see the girls as dots below me by the large white hanger, but this was the first time I had seen the horizon, with the remnants of a city in the distance, and the navy blue, sparkling sea beyond that.

"Ok," I thought.

"The aeroplane can hover, but what's it like flying forwards?"

I touched the controls to slowly rotate the engines to face backwards instead of downwards and our flying machine started flying forwards, quite slowly at first.

Dad flying the Family Flyer.

A few seconds later and I was in full forward flight, heading towards the frothing white lines of waves at the coast.

I pulled the joystick to go left and then right, upwards, and downwards.

I did some low ground passes over dead trees and dried grass, all the while the rust-coloured dust I created blew vortexes all around.

Then I did a complete three sixty celebratory roll once I was at four thousand feet.

I was more than happy with how responsive our new machine was, and what the airplane could do.

I touched the "home" button on the screen and the Flyer did a complete backward loop, upside down.

I felt I was riding on a large roller coaster, until I finally headed for home, landing automatically outside the large white hanger, with the two girls jumping for joy, hugging each other.

I switched the engines off and stepped out of the aircraft to join in a group hug.

I felt this was truly a new start, a new beginning for the airplane and our family.

For that reason, and also partly in remembrance of the family who lost their lives in the yellow Piper plane crash at the entrance to the bunker, there was absolutely no doubt in my mind what we were going to name our new aeroplane.

"The Family Flyer".

Skye and the Flyer.

CHAPTER 2

Martin the Messenger.

The very next day we took the "Family Flyer" out for a spin. Once again Skye wanted to pilot the craft, and I had no problem with that, in fact I encouraged it, even when Kat looked at me in a disapproving way as if to say,"Is it right to give a 16-year-old girl so much responsibility - put our lives in her hands"?

I knew very well that Skye was no ordinary sixteen-year-old girl.

She was tough physically, practising her martial arts, Yoga or working out in the gym nearly every day, but also, she was like a twenty-two-year-old emotionally, morally and mentally.

I guess this was because she spent so much time with her Mum and me, with no other children around to distract or influence her the last three years.

I guess you might even say that's a little bit sad, because she mostly was serious about everything she did, about the people in her life, and her ideas for the future.

Maybe this was what made her such a strong, fearless, focused personality and such a great pilot at such a young age.

It took just seconds to become airborne, taking off from outside the large white hanger, and just a few minutes more before the three of us were flying at about two thousand feet following the coastline.

The houses below were dilapidated, boats were abandoned and strewn about but the coastal path looked surprisingly well maintained, devoid of debris, litter or overgrown foliage.

Then I saw the reason for the good condition of the path.

Something humanoid, or was it a man, or was it an android, was running at a fair pace along the path.

Martin the Messenger.

I spoke into the aeroplane's communication system.

"Skye, honey, take us down to check that out please."

I pointed down and to the right below us. Skye knew what I meant immediately as she could see a dust cloud coming from the object that was moving fast along the coastal path.

It was the first sight of life outside our home we had seen for three years.

We never saw a bird fly, or a stray cat or dog, or any cattle or any insects but did come across a variety of animal carcasses.

Once we even found a dead tiger in the dry shrubbery, where the family crashed their yellow Piper aeroplane.

Maybe its keeper released it from a zoo in the city to give it a fighting chance for survival on its own, but it obviously did not make it. I quickly caught up, and circled the speeding object, to find it was a man running in an exoskeleton suit.

It made him look quite robotic, but enhanced his abilities and particularly, his running speed, allowing him to run for longer, at a fast pace, without becoming tired.

"Why was this sole runner going through all this effort?" I asked myself.

We headed for a wider space a couple of hundred meters in front of him and landed. He stopped running to meet the Family Flyer and to say, "Hi."

"What are you doing? Why the running?" I asked, stepping down off the "Family Flyer".

"I'm Martin the Messenger," he said pointing to a red, white and green badge on his chest which read, "Martin's Messengers".

I hadn't thought about it until that very moment, but I should have realised that communication between pockets of people these days would be a problem and could even be a business of some kind.

We had taken it for granted that our Wi-Fi system, generated by the Flyers' router, was so easy to set up and use. This was backed up by a radio system.

Martin the messenger was doing what the Greeks and Romans did hundreds of years before the destruction - he was personally carrying a written or verbal message from one place to the other.

Landing the Family Flyer at the University.

"How often do you deliver messages?" I asked Martin.

"Every couple of days if I feel fit enough, and if the suit holds out."

"Where are you headed?
Maybe we can help take you there." I gestured to the aeroplane.

Martin's face lit up and he quickly set about removing his Exo suit.

It was not long before we pulled the door-stairs up and took off again, with Martin sitting in one of the rear seats with Kat, both behind me.

"This airplane is seriously impressive", he said, looking around the cockpit area and inspecting the adjoining toilet and living room.

We followed the coastal path, that he ran most days, for a good hour and a half before Martin gestured to head down to some interesting Gothic buildings, with one which was the university campus quad.

We aimed the Family Flyer for the middle, hovered gracefully, doing a full three sixty horizontal rotation and as she did so, people started emerging from every building, heading towards us.

Some people were in soldier's uniforms, and carried guns aimed threateningly at us, but as soon as they saw Martin waving at them through the large cockpit windows, they began to relax and smile and sling their rifles back over their shoulders and started waving back.

The aircraft's engines stopped and everyone seemed happy to see the aeroplane and us. I soon realised that they had been holed up, just like we had been, in the basement car parks and other protected parts of the campus for as long as we had.

We were the first outsiders they had seen in three years.

The leader, a tall skinny man with a bow-tie, balding head and glasses, shook our hands vigorously one by one, introducing himself as Dean Grey. The Dean was in charge of the whole college.

"Welcome, welcome. Come and have a coffee.

Have you eaten? Tell me where you have come from, and what is this fabulous flying machine you came in?"

Dean Grey is taken Hostage.

Entering the university cafeteria seemed to me to be so natural and yet so strange. Young people sat eating their lunch or sipping their coffees, teas and hot chocolates whilst staring into their books or writing in note pads while armed guards stood in the doorways or paced about.

Students were being stopped outside and their bags searched by uniformed soldiers with guns before they were allowed into the cafeteria. I asked Dean Grey about the high security measures and he explained.

"Since the day of destruction, when we moved down into the basement shelters, we have been attacked twice. The first was a lone gunman with a Kalashnikov machine gun who just opened up in the assembly hall killing seven students, three staff and two soldiers.

It was a bloody scene quite incomprehensible considering what the world had just been through and how the human race has had to resort to living like rats underground to survive.

He was eventually shot dead by the armed soldiers.

We discovered later he still had affiliations with radical religious fanatics even though the group existed no more.

The second attack was a gradual poisoning by one of the ladies on the kitchen staff.

She was putting a small amount of poison into the food each day which made many people sick very slowly and unfortunately, she killed one of our students.

We never found out if she was affiliated with any of the terrorist groups or whether she was just someone who was a disturbed individual who was acting alone.

We finally caught her antics on CCTV which led to her leaving the university campus in a hurry never to be seen again.

She probably died on the road after a few days as she did not leave the university campus wearing a safe suit or a mask.

Coincidently, or maybe due to our overheard conversation, a student, wearing lipstick, makeup and a Marc Bolan tee shirt, moved closer to the Dean.

At first glance the student looked female, and stood unnervingly close behind Dean Grey. Something was telling me that all was not quite right which was confirmed a moment later when a chrome plated, automatic pistol was suddenly produced and placed up against Dean Grey's temple.

The student pulled Dean Grey backwards and down onto a dining chair.

Banshee throwing the gun.

The Dean was visibly shaking with fear as I think anyone would be in that situation.

I said as calmly as I could to the cross-dressed student, "What is this all about.

What do you want?"

She said, "I need to get out of here now-today."

"Ok, I said you're talking to the right person," I said, holding my hands up, trying to make light of a tense situation.

"I've got the Family Flyer just outside and you only had to ask.

Come on put down the gun."

I could see from the corner of my eye two soldiers were pointing their rifles at the student and their red laser dots now danced on the student's body from chest to head and back again.

"Come on please, put the gun down before you get yourself shot," I said, worryingly.

In an instant she replied, "Here take it," she said, throwing the gun at me.

"It's not even loaded anyway", she said.

She tossed the gun my way, pushing Dean Grey forwards.

She was right, it was just a replica air pellet gun.

I said, "You could have gotten yourself killed over this silly prank".

"I don't care anymore, I can't stay here.

I'm going crazy", she said.

I was interested to see what was going to happen next.

Was Dean Grey going to have this student expelled, arrested, banished or possibly even, shot?

Banshee Playing Piano.

Dean Grey just sat down still shaking and said, "Stephen Foxley, you should be ashamed of yourself upsetting your uncle like that and wearing that - that - stuff on your face."

Stephen answered aggressively, looking in my direction, "You see, I told you all before. I'm not Stephen Foxley anymore.

I'm Banshee.

Not Banshee Foxley or Stephen.

Banshee, is my name - just Banshee. It's more than my nickname or a stage name it's my actual new name now.

So, come on Uncle Harry are you arresting me or not?",

Banshee said to her uncle Dean Grey holding her wrists together above her head as if she was handcuffed.

"Oh, away with you - you foolish boy...girl...person", the Dean answered.

"Hurray, I'm free", Banshee started singing and what a terrific voice she had.

"I'm free, I'm free as a bird in the s-k-y-i -i.

Free as a bird oh, yeah".

She quickly made her way to the piano and started playing and continued singing.

People were laughing at first and not quite sure what to make of the scene but started crowding around her, all the same, and it seemed like the tension of a few moments ago had completely dissipated.

Even the soldiers, who moments ago, were pointing their guns towards her were now tapping their feet to Banshee's song.

A student sat down at the drums and another plugged her guitar in to the amplifier to accompany Banshee.

It was not long before Banshee had everyone in the cafeteria up on their feet dancing and singing along while she played the piano and sang.

In the days following, the singing sessions in the cafeteria became more regular.

It started at lunchtime and continued on from there through dinner time and beyond.

Dad & Banshee talking about music.

During a pause in one of the singing sessions, Banshee came and sat at a table opposite me.

She said, "You kept it very quiet - Jack Ezra - Weekend Daddy".

I had not heard those words for over fifteen years and with the war, divorce and a new family, it seemed like my musical career ended a few lifetimes ago.

Banshee looked straight into my eyes and grinned a huge grin like a cat who had just found the cream and waited for an answer.

I said, "Yep, it's no secret that I made a few music albums, some time ago.

The first was called "Premonition", the second was called "Weekend Daddy" and the third was called "Watching My Six" with a single called "Ibiza Ibiza".

Why do you ask?", I said.

"Your music is really cool, Jack Ezra.

Do you mind if I do some of your songs", Banshee asked?

"I don't think the songs from Weekend Daddy are really relevant to you guys as that music album was dedicated to Fathers who were forcibly split away from their children and only saw them on weekends."

"I want to do your songs - Maybe the Ibiza one or the UFO one from the Watching My Six, album," Banshee asked.

"UFO's Are Real - Yeah sure, no problem", I said, my mind racing ahead.

"You love music, Banshee, and you also want to get out of here. Is that right?

"Yes, she said", without any hesitation.

"OK, then", I replied, " I might just have an idea for you....."

Over the following few days Banshee gathered a team of students and other individuals who might have liked to accompany her on a new adventure.

Landing the Family Flyer on the roof of the radio station.

The new plan was that we were going to locate her and her followers in the abandoned radio station building in the outskirts of the main city about a four-hour flight from the university or a day by road.

It was my idea to rejuvenate the station with people and get the radio station back on the air.

I would fly the Family Flyer with Banshee, Helen, her friend, and Skye and try to get the building generator going while the others, including Kat and some technicians and some of Banshee's fans would make their way by road using the university minibus.

I hugged and kissed Kat goodbye and said see you in a couple of days and off we flew up and over the college grounds back towards the mountains.

All of the college came out to wave us off and Banshee waved, hugged and kissed many of her admirers acting like some kind of pop superstar.

I could not quite put my finger on why this was such a special moment but maybe it was that this was a reminder of how people acted and how things were before the war - before the lock-down - a glimmer of hope of a new life and getting back to a kind of normality.

It was the first venture away from the safety of the college by these young people so it meant a great deal to them and very soon we were up four thousand feet watching the parched earth below.

We talked, laughed, slept, ate, drank listened to music and made jokes throughout the four-hour flight, landing on the roof of the radio station building just as the sun was setting, was a beautiful, tranquil and warm evening, the suns orange and pink rays washed the pale blue sky while, here and there, fluffy white clouds were tinted with the glorious colours of evening.

It was hard to think of our world as dead or dying but my brain, knew, the thirty or so story, building below our feet was nothing more than a rusting, damp and most likely, hazardous place, to venture into.

Breaking open the door to the stairwell.

Once landed, I broke open the roof door with a crowbar with Skye, Banshee and Helen, following noiselessly, close behind me.

I knew the sound studios were most likely near the top of the building so we would not have too far to go.

The stairs were dark and smelled really badly of damp and we had to use our torches. The stairs were wet with condensation and it was like walking on slippery ice. Just two quick flights down and through a doorway and we entered the more respectable, dry and clean corridor, which led to the sound studios and some offices.

We entered through the heavy soundproof double doors displaying an unlit sign saying, "Studio 4" and once inside we were confronted with a beautiful glossy, black, grand piano and musical instruments and guitar and bass amplifiers all around.

The picture windows now framed the beautiful silhouetted and abandoned buildings of this forgotten city.

The dark grey shapes of the buildings were blank and lifeless with not a light on as far as the eye could see.

I suddenly felt very lonely until Skye tapped me on the shoulder bringing me back down to earth.

"Dad, should we go and sort the generator out while Banshee and Helen set up camp here".

I nodded and said, " Okay, but we could be a while as it's probably in the basement about thirty floors or more down the stairs."

The others nodded and gave a thumbs up and Skye and I set off back down the dark and smelly stairwell while
Helen and Banshee started unpacking the Family Flyer of their musical equipment and luggage.

Lit by our hand torches, Skye and I carefully began our descent down thirty floors to the basement which was flooded, waist high in muddy water.

We reluctantly waded across the basement towards where the generator stood, which luckily was just above the flood line.

There seemed to be gasoline in it and a couple of turns on a small hand crank was all that it took to start the motor.

A couple of seconds later and the basement lights, lift and all the equipment in the studios in the whole building came to life.

The monster in the Basement.

"What was that", Skye yelled.

"Dad, something just brushed past my leg.

There's something in here-swimming around in the water with us".

I thought there was little or no chance of any animals being alive as the radiation and toxins after the bomb strikes killed everything, but I wasn't planning to find out.

"Skye, let's get out of this soup and get back upstairs".

I turned to face Skye and rearing, a metre above her head and behind her, was a giant snake dragon monster.

It's neck, almost a foot wide and fangs, sharp and long.

It's eyes matched the red colour of its black and deep red, scales.

It swished the remainder of its long, strong body in the muddy water and raised its head even higher ready to strike a death blow at my unaware daughter.

I waited for a second and as the snake-dragon's head started to come down, I dived at Skye's body in a rugby tackle forcibly moving her sideways out of the path of the snake's death blow.

Underwater, I could see Skye's face was stunned and surprised as to what her Father was doing.

I grabbed her waistband and pulled her away swimming as hard as I could, to the side of the room.

There was lots of debris on the basement floor but more importantly, I spotted a manhole cover which I was hoping was a drain.

I pointed it out to Skye, beckoning her to help me remove it and without question, she grabbed the other handle on the manhole cover and we both pulled at it with all our might.

Suddenly the cover came off and I could feel the water pulling us in towards the drain so we swam in the opposite direction, to the side of the room and grabbed hold of a window ledge.

After catching our breath for a moment Skye looked at me as if to say, "What's going on Dad," but she did not have to wait very long for her answer.

In the middle of the room the snake–dragon was being sucked into the drain tail first.

Insects in the arm before taking the elevator.

It thrashed around for a while making a couple of fruitless lunges in our direction but the water was going down extremely fast taking the monster with it.

We saw its head snarling in our direction for a moment and suddenly, as swiftly as I spotted the danger, the water and the snake-dragon were gone and it was all quiet, leaving just the sound of dripping and trickling water and the hum of the generator in the background.

Without a word, and an arm around Skye, we headed out of the basement towards the now, active service lift shaft.

"Ding-dong", and a minute later we were exiting the lift on the twenty eighth floor.

Covered in slimy mud and dripping wet, I had not noticed until then, the insect larvae wriggling under the skin of my left forearm.

"Now what", I muttered to myself.

"What's wrong, Dad", Skye asked. I held up my arm and showed her.
Four or five ant shape, insects were grouped together in a blister just under the skin of my forearm.

I could clearly see the shapes of their heads, body's and even their eyes.

"We need to get them out, Dad," Skye said urgently.

"Let me see", Helen piped up, walking out of the sound studio to greet us.

After all she was studying medicine and training to be a doctor.

"Hmm," she said quietly to herself.

"Haven't seen this type of insect infestation before but I do know that we need to get them out from under your skin asap.

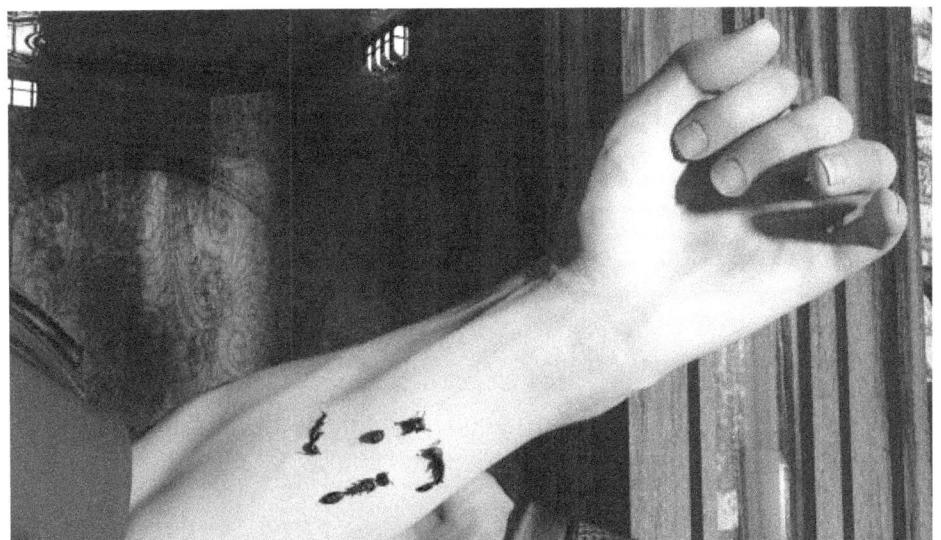

The only building with lights on in the City.

They look like some kind of deformed, modified ant".
I simply nodded in agreement.

It wasn't long before she pulled a medical pack from her backpack and sprayed my forearm with a local anaesthetic spray.

I couldn't watch while Helen slit the skin on my forearm and with tweezers, pulled each insect out one by one from the sticky puss filled bubble.

Meanwhile, I had a small and very vocal audience.

Skye was making being sick noises while Banshee could not get close enough to take a look, saying, " Wow, look at these bad boys".

Helen dropped all four insects into a cup and said, "Do you want to keep them for the college science lab or should we dispose of them."

I said, "Get rid of them. They're horrible."

"I think I'll keep them for my studies," Helen said, disagreeing with me.

Camping down for the night was quick, easy and efficient as we were all so exhausted and I did take a moment to gaze out of the window.

I was going to sleep in the main bedroom of the Family Flyer up on the roof and Skye bunked down in the bedroom next door to me but just before turning out the bedside lamp I noticed that our building was the only one with lights on in the whole city and I wondered if there was anyone else out there and if they could see the Radio Tower station sign all lit up on the roof.

The next day saw all kinds of normality being introduced into our lives.

We found a fully equipped kitchen with a larder full of canned food.

We also found a freezer with rotting carcasses which smelled terrible, however we could clean it out and use it at some point in the future but Banshee was determined to begin the rehearsals and recording of my songs.

I was kind of flattered that she was so keen to do this so in one of the studios I started laying down the tracks on the computer one by one and she was absolutely loving every second of the whole experience.

Rehearsing and recording songs.

Skye and Helen would pop in to hear how we were getting on and for meals between exploring the other floors of the building.

Every few hours that went by I would be in touch with Kathleen and from time to time I would track her with the "Find My" iPhone app to see her exact position.

Before long we managed to record a couple of songs and we even found the music publishing department on the twelfth floor which stored millions of songs, artists documentaries, videos and movies.

We simply had to work out how to start transmitting, and working the radio equipment.

That evening, after dinner, and all of us in a happy mood, Helen suddenly collapsed onto my lap.

There were plenty of other seats in the studio control room and I hadn't realised until that moment, how stunningly attractive she was with her short blond bob hairstyle.

She was wearing a short, flowered, cotton, mini dress with black leggings and her long legs straddled my lap provocatively.

I was surprised but totally enjoying the moment until I heard myself say,

"There are plenty of other seats, Helen."

"Oh, alright - be like that then", she responded and off she shot.

I did not want to hurt her feelings but I felt guilty about something.

Maybe it was that I did find her attractive and would have loved to get to know her more intimately even though she was many years younger than I, but all I could think about was if I took any relationship forwards to the next stage it would upset Skye, who was right there across the room and my wife Kat, would be really hurt.

I guess my subconscious kicked in and decided in an instant to shut the whole episode down before it ever had a chance to begin.

Mum questions Dad about Helen.

The next day did see the arrival of the college minibus, amongst who were technicians who began work immediately on getting the radio station on the air.

For me it was wonderful to see Kat again.

Maybe it was the way I kissed or hugged my wife that made her ask suspiciously, looking in Helen's direction,

"What's the matter, honey.

What've you been up to?"

"Nothing, actually. Just happy to see you", I answered.

Two days later the radio station was operational thanks to the technical help.

They would have to manage the filling up of the backup electricity generator in the basement from time to time but that was easily solved with several gas stations in and around the area.

Skye and I went with two others, back into the basement and checked the drain but there was no sign of the snake-dragon so a couple of the technicians welded the drain cover shut just to make sure it did not return.

Banshee was a natural and terrific disc jockey and became the voice of the radio station.

Others soon learned how to become radio presenters and how to use the music library and before too long I was beginning to feel redundant and looking to say farewell and leave them all to it.

Helen had a choice of several, young, handsome lads to spend time with and within twenty-four hours Kat and Skye

The University Cemetery.

Once there, the next two days were spent visiting all the habitable parts of the university, and talking to everyone about how they lived and where we lived, what they had experienced and what we had seen, and our plans for "Freedom Point" and our plans to try to find our son, Jimi Jack.

Our last stop was the cemetery located just outside the college, which was a sea of white crosses, stars of David and tombstones.

There must have been thousands of graves there, which brought home the horror of death that the war and the virus had brought and that had not long passed.

Martin brought over another messenger who said he knew of a couple of tribes with a lot of children and teenagers who lived a few hundred kilometres North West of the university, and we should fly there next.

I thought that was a good idea.

I thanked Dean Grey, Martin and everyone else but, most importantly, I left them some cell phones, chargers and radio equipment to keep in touch with us now that cell phone and data reception was nearly back to normal.

Martin the Messenger and his friend would be more than happy to give up their message delivery running business, jobs and to be using the phones and radio equipment for communication, instead.

Dad & Dean Grey on phones.

I thought the future had to have a better communication network than messenger runners so I guess I started the ball rolling by calling Dean Grey on one of the iPhones from the cockpit as we took off, much to the delight of the other bystanders.

"Hi, Dean Grey, can you hear me okay?", I said into an iPhone which had not seen the light of day for a long time.

"Yes, yes, I can hear you loud and clear," he replied excitedly.

"This is probably the first cell phone call in three years," I said, "Yes, it's wonderful.

I wish you lots of luck in finding your son, Jimi Jack."

"Thank you, Dean Grey. Until next time then...bye for now."

As I finished our conversation, I hoped Dean Grey's good luck wish would help us find our son.

View From Right

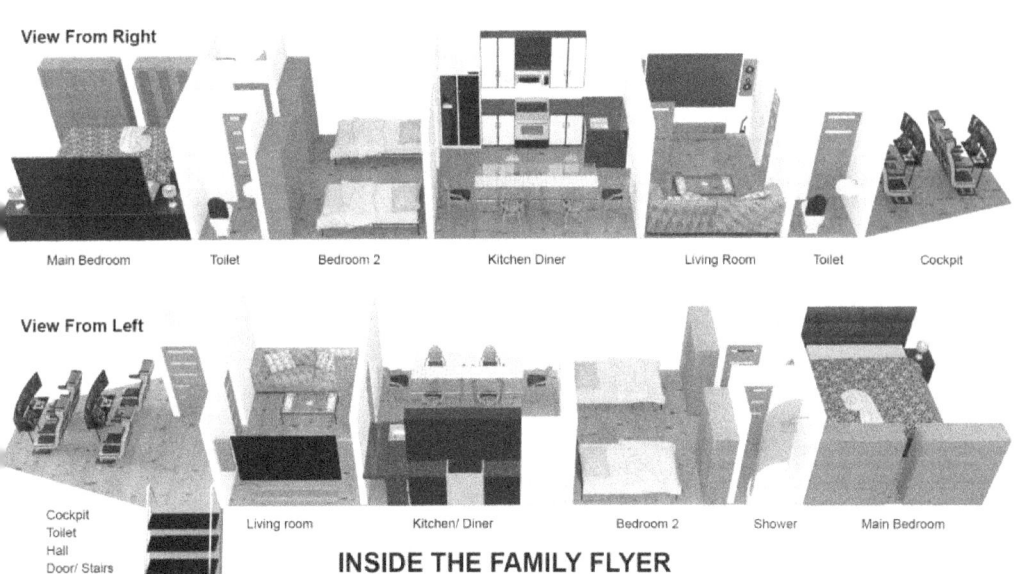

Main Bedroom   Toilet   Bedroom 2   Kitchen Diner   Living Room   Toilet   Cockpit

View From Left

Cockpit
Toilet
Hall
Door/ Stairs

Living room   Kitchen/ Diner   Bedroom 2   Shower   Main Bedroom

INSIDE THE FAMILY FLYER

The Boomerang Beast spots the Family Flyer.

CHAPTER 003—The Boomerang Beast.

The Boomerang Beast raised his large boomerang high up over his head to gain the attention of the group of children.

The painted skull on the boomerang, a reminder, of his terrible strength and power while his three-pronged spear rested firmly in his left hand and glinted in the sun from time to time.

There must have been about fifty children ranging in age from six to sixteen.
The older ones looked menacing standing next to their leader, the Boomerang Beast.

Silence swept across the group like a tsunami wave until even the smallest child was quiet and still.

"Today we lost Nathan and Rob to the Biter Clan", the Beast boomed out from on top of the high rock.

There was a sigh throughout the group of children.

Some of the younger ones started to whimper.

"Stop that", the Beast commanded.

"We are going to get them back.

We are never going to let that happen to any more of us.

We are going to fortify. We are going to defend, and we are going to stop this ever happening again."

As the crowd cheered, nodding in agreement with the Beast's emotional words, an object partially obscured the sun, casting a shadow over the whole group, which made them fall silent once again.

They all turned around and looked up. It was the Family Flyer, coming in slowly from the direction of the sun.

The group, now in silence, seemed uncertain how to react.

The Beast reassured them, calling out, "Be still.
It is just a flying machine—an aeroplane, and I believe they are friendly."

The Family Flyer came in closer and closer, hovered for a moment over the group, and settled to the side kicking up whirlwinds of dry, golden dust as it landed.

Two figures emerged from the airplane wearing pristine flight suits, with full respirator masks covering their faces.

They were Kat and myself.

Meeting the Boomerang Beast and the Wrang-a-tang clan.

We removed our gas masks as Skye watched through one of the cockpit windows.

The group of male teenagers, armed with various hand weapons, stood menacingly, in a circle around us.

The Boomerang Beast, in full protective gear, stood silent and motionless for a moment, then slowly removed his helmet and called out, "Mum, Dad.

 I can't believe it."
"Jimi Jack," Kat and I screamed in unison.

We ran to him and he ran to us.
We hugged one another for a long time.

We had hoped for this moment for so many long months and we were surely going to savour it for as long as we could.

By now the group had gathered around the aeroplane.

They had never seen a flying machine like the Family Flyer before - actually, no one had.

The Beast introduced the strangers.
"Everyone, I am so happy to introduce you to my Mother and Father".

Everyone clapped, and the older ones near the Beast patted him on the back and gave him high fives.

Of course, some of the younger ones did not even remember what a Mother and Father were.

They could not understand what the Boomerang Beast was so joyful about.

I said to my son, putting a friendly arm around him, "Come on, I have a nice surprise for you".

I led him inside the Flyer.

I walked a few steps and alarm bells started to ring inside my head.

There were bare footprints all around the door stairs and into the cockpit where Skye had been waiting.

There was no sign of my daughter, just dusty, scuff marks and a partially open cabin door.

I had planned to show Jimi Jack his little sister all grown up and a pilot, but now she was gone.

Jimi Jack knelt down and closely examined the footprints all around the airplane and in the dry dirt outside the airplane.

Skye has been taken.

"The Biter Clan have been here.

They have taken Skye just as they did two others of our clan, he said quietly.

Kat was by my side with her hand to her mouth.

Removing it slowly she said in a worried voice, " What does this mean, Jimi Jack? Can we go after her, and the others?"

"Don't worry, Mum.

Well get her back with Nathan and Rob".

The Boomerang Beast, the leader of the "Wrang-a-tang clan" was Jimi Jack our long-lost son and he began to explain the intricacies of the situation.

"The Biter Clan live across the water.

They have rafts, as they have fruit and many trees on their side of the water."

"We can't swim across because the water is contaminated and radioactive, so we can't cross, but they can cross over to our side whenever they want to".

"Yes, but now you have the Family Flyer", I said, to my son, placing my hand gently on the grey metal of the airplane.

Jimi Jack nodded in agreement, taking in the ramifications of us being able to use the aeroplane.

"How many can you carry, Dad?", he asked.

Crossing the contaminated, radioactive river.

"It's only a short hop over the river so quite a few, I guess", I replied.

After some preparation we lifted off with Kat and I, Jimi Jack and another older boy dressed in green, in the cockpit seats while others were spread out throughout the aeroplane, in the living room, kitchen and the bedrooms, making a total of seventeen in all.

I could feel the Family Flyer's engines straining with the extra weight of the children and could see and hear the wings bending and creaking with the strain, but we lifted off, flew to an altitude of just ten feet and headed for the silvery, sparkling, but deadly, river.

It took only twelve seconds or so to cross the gleaming, water before we landed on the "Biter Clan's" side.

We all disembarked very quickly, our helpers carrying thick branches, knives, axes and even a crossbow, for weapons.

I remotely piloted the empty aeroplane back over to the other side of the water with my iPad as a precaution and followed the others into the woods.

It was only moments before we came across human skeletons which had been deliberately left in the water or hung from trees, or propped against fences.

I did notice that it was much greener here than anywhere else we had been to and there was also a curious and powerful stench that made us all want to throw up.

Jimi Jack explained, "They say this clan are cannibals.

As it is too dangerous to eat contaminated fruit, vegetables or animals, they eat each other, and other people if they can catch them."

On hearing this Kat burst into sobs.

"No, it's ok, Mum, we've never known of anyone actually been eaten, or even being hurt by the Biter Clan, but we can't take that chance, and we always get everyone back in the end."

Mati and the Biter Clan.

"How long has this been going on?" I asked.

"Since the very beginning when I joined them just after the bombs hit", Jimi Jack explained.

There was no food for anyone.

We were all one gang to start with until some of the girls decided to live across the water—in the woods," Jimi Jack continued.

Suddenly the ground gave way beneath some of our team who were walking ahead.

They had fallen through a trap - a thin layer of twigs covered in leaves and grass, into a pit about three meters deep.

One or two of the boys lay motionless, while others moaned or clutched their ankles, or backs, in pain.

I quickly threw down a knotted rope which I had placed in a backpack earlier with the iPad, and assisted the fitter teenagers to climb back up to our level, but the others just gestured for us to keep going without them.

Up ahead I could see blue smoke rising from a small campfire which twisted this way and that in the warm wind, and the stench of rotting flesh was almost too much to bear.

A figure stood motionless, ahead carrying a basket of apples.

Was it male or female, young or old?

I was not sure, but what I was sure about was a strange chattering sound growing all around our group.

"It's okay," Jimi Jack said.

"It's their strange way of letting us know that they are there, and that we are surrounded.

It's their teeth - they chomp them together to make that sound.

Trying to frighten us."

"They're doing a good job," Kat said, holding on to two of the younger boys who were looking a little frightened.

Before long we were face to face with a figure by an open fire, which we guessed was the Biter Clan's leader, Matilda or Mati as she was known to some, and a number of other girls of varying ages stood all around her.

Mati and the Boomerang Beast have a confrontation.

Suddenly, and from every side, our group was pelted with a hail of foul-smelling gunk. It consisted of excrement, putrid vegetation and decomposing flesh.

Some of this stinking slop was alive with maggots which crawled through our hair and clung to our clothes.

The overwhelming stench was enough to make the members of our party double up and throw up instantly, all except for Jimi Jack who was well protected from the slop, in his fearsome, armoured, protective suit.

The Biter Clan used this sickening concoction as a powerful aroma weapon and within the few seconds that we were uncontrollably, being sick, several of them descended upon us, surrounded us, and bound our hands together behind our backs, taking us prisoner.

One or two of our group who were unaffected by the stench, tried to defend themselves for a few moments, but they were soon overpowered by the sheer numbers of the Biter Clan girls descending upon them.

Kat and I struggled at first to get away but more and more of them just kept coming, each one holding on to a part of us until we were overpowered and could not move.

Then we heard a huge booming voice explode like thunder, from the fearsome warrior who was our son, the Boomerang Beast.

"ENOUGH, I say, enough," he roared.

The Boomerang Beast slowly raised his extra-large, fearsomely decorated, boomerang to the sky, and the leader of the Biter Clan raised a spear.

BB and Mati arguing.

Everyone stood still, and both groups fell silent.

The Biter Clan's leader spoke first, "Why do you invade our land this side of the river?"

Matilda was a slender girl, older than the others, who wore an army utility belt with her face always covered in black, red and white war paint.

"We have come to get back our people," the Boomerang Beast said in a loud voice, addressing both gangs.

"We do not have your people," the Biter Clan's leader argued.

"Yes, they do," Kat and I heard on our radio earpieces, simultaneously.

It was Skye, speaking from somewhere nearby, as she could also hear what was being said between the two leaders.

"Where are you, honey?" Kat spoke quietly into her mouthpiece.

"I'm in a pit somewhere nearby.

Hold on, I'm going to push a branch through.

There, can you see this?"

Mati attacks with her spear.

About a hundred yards behind, and off to the right of the two leaders, a branch was waving back and forth.

"We see you," both Kat and I called out together, but before I could move, and in what seemed like a split second, Mati's sharp, silver pointed spear was at my neck.

"Please, I just want my daughter back," I said, thinking that was going to help.

The point of the spear now piercing my skin and causing a small trickle of blood to run down my neck.

"Enough," the Boomerang Beast, exploded, once again, knocking the spear to the ground in one swift and powerful blow.

"Excuse us, we have a daughter to rescue," I said, whipping the knotted rope from my shoulder as I ran over to where Skye was trapped.

Kat joined me seconds later, helping to remove twigs and leaves from the pit's roof.

There were two other children in the square pit with Skye and I guessed they were Nathan and Rob.

Skye and Mati fight.

CHAPTER 004 - The Apple Orchard.

"Hi, honey", I said to Skye.

"I'll have all of you out as quick as I can", I said, hurriedly, tying one end of the knotted rope to a sturdy tree, and lowering the other end down into the pit.

The two younger children climbed onto Skye, and she climbed up out of the muddy pit into the sunlight.

Skye saw the leader of the Biter Clan, as her eyes adjusted to the more intense light after emerging from the pit.

Placing the two children down carefully, she brushed off the remaining mud from her flight-suit and started walking briskly and purposefully, towards the leader of the Biter Clan.

Skye was not smiling, in fact the nearer she came to Matilda the more her face seemed sterner until she was just a couple of metres from her.

The leader of the biter Clan sensed that something was wrong and quickly turned to face Skye changing her footing and her stance and pointed her spear towards Skye in readiness for an attack.

She was right to do so as the attack from Skye came just a second later with a roundhouse kick to the Biter Clan leaders' head.

The girl took the blow quite well recoiling slightly but bringing the shaft of the spear down on Skye's head with a crack followed by another blow with the blunt end of the spear right into Skye's stomach.

Skye took this blow well and came back with a barrage of punches to the leader's face, head and stomach.

This stunned the leader for a moment and that's when Skye came in for the kill.

She pounced on to the leaders back bringing her down on the ground and in an instant wrapped her legs around the leader's neck in a strangle hold until the Biter Clan's leader was gasping for breath trying to pull Skye's leg away from her neck.

Testing Apples.

By now both clans were standing round in a wide circle watching the fight with a few of the Biter Clan members looking quite upset.

Just as the Boomerang Beast was about to step in and pull Skye off the leader, and before she did some real damage, I dropped down to ground level and addressed the fighting pair.

"Skye, honey I know you are upset about being kidnapped and thrown in a muddy pit, but can you please, please, release Matilda, now."

Skye did not look too happy about my suggestion but released her grip on the leader all the same.

I pulled out a chocolate bar from my backpack and offered it to the fearsome leader of the Biter Clan.

I said, "Please take this.

Open it - eat it - it's really good."

The leader took the candy bar from me, stood up and then unwrapped the chocolate bar slowly removing the wrapper and taking a delicious bite.

She smiled a big chocolaty smile at us and I knew at that very moment that this was the start of something new, positive and good for the two warring Clans.

Just then two children carrying baskets of apples emerged from the thickly wooded undergrowth.

"Wait, you have fruit? Is it safe to eat?" I asked, removing a toxicity tester from my pocket.

I checked a couple of apples in one basket, then I did the same with an apple from the other basket.

I grabbed one, tossing it in the air, and took a large, delicious bite out of it and passed a couple more apples to Skye and Kat who bit into their apples enthusiastically.

"Perfectly safe and really nice," I said.

"What I don't understand is where you are getting the uncontaminated water from, because the stream we crossed over is not usable".

The Bridge.

Jimi Jack came closer to listen as Matilda, the Biter Clan's leader, answered.

"There is an underground stream which comes out in the apple orchard."

"With that we can grow all the fruit and vegetables we need.

We can wash and cook with the water, and it's safe to drink", Mati explained.

This was quite something, I thought.

If I hadn't carefully stored several tankers of water back at Freedom Point, we could not have survived three years of lockdown.

To have a limitless supply of drinkable water was incredibly precious and very lucky.

"So how are we going to resolve your differences?" I said to the Boomerang Beast and Matilda.

"We can move to this side of the water and help you farm - try to live together in peace," the Boomerang Beast, suggested.

Kat looked at me and then on to the two teenagers and I could see the pride in her face that this was our son talking in such a grown-up, sensible way.

I also knew from Kats face that she was worried that there might be a romance brewing here and that Jimi Jack might not be coming with us when we left the two Clans.

"Well, I for one think it's a terrific idea that both Clans work and live together from now on - pool your resources".

"Together you are much stronger," I said. "We just have to fix up a safe way of crossing the water back and forth, easily."

"It could be a line stretched across, or a floating ferry pulled by ropes or maybe even build a bridge", I suggested, putting an arm around Jimi Jack and Matilda's shoulders, either side of me, and walked them over towards the water's edge to take a closer look at the problem.

I also noticed them giving each other lots of sideways glances with smiles from Matilda.

Within days, a sturdy wooden bridge was built.

The Flyer was used to stretch ropes across the water and to ferry people, tools, wood and supplies back and forth.

The Clan Leaders were now the best of Friends.

A few more days passed and everyone was feeling very smug that there was a sturdy, wooden bridge across the poisonous water and peace and a friendly atmosphere between the Clans, had been created.

It was wonderful to see children from both sides playing together and admiring each other's efforts and the sound of joyful laughter was something neither Clan had heard for a long time.

However, I was concerned that Jimi Jack and Matilda seemed to be growing closer day by day.

Funny how two leaders who constantly distrusted each other were now the best of friends.

It almost looked like they were planning for a life together.

This was going to be hard for Kat and I because our plans involved taking Jimi Jack back with us.

Life would be just a little more comfortable for the two tribes now, but how would we convince our son to come with us and leave his new girlfriend behind?

"We're planning to leave in the morning," I heard Kat say to our son. "What are your plans, Jimi Jack"?

"Mum, it's terrific to see you guys, and I really thought I would never see you again, but I am needed here, and also I want to be with Matilda."

"I'm so proud of you," Kat said with tears running down her cheeks. "You have turned out to be such a responsible and caring young man, and I fully understand why you want to stay here. I'm going to miss you so much."

Kat hugged her son and kissed him on the cheek as if to say goodbye forever, and turned towards me, looking really sad, with tears streaming down her face.

The Boomerang Beast walked off towards Matilda, who was waiting by the tree line.

Both teenagers, with broad smiles on their faces, walked off together, hand in hand, into the woods with everyone else looking on wondering what was going to happen now that the two clan leaders looked like they were the best of friends.

Somewhere above our heads Skye was in the Family Flyer. She had deployed Drone 111 to track what was going on in the orchard.

We often deployed our drones to assist monitoring whatever situation we were in.

Monitoring drone video in the Family Flyer's Living Room.

Skye monitored her brother with Matilda, Mati's girls, the lads and Kat and I, collecting apples, all from the comfort of the airplane's cockpit.

That night, when we were asleep in bed an alarm went off warning us that something or someone was close to the Family Flyer.

It turned out to be some of the children, who then started banging on the aircraft back door, which was our bedroom, and they were shouting.

"Wake up, wake up. The Boomerang Beast has gone mad and he is destroying the new bridge."

Kat lowered the back door to greet the children while I set-off two drones, "Triple One" and "Triple Two", to investigate what was going on.

One drone was to go directly to the bridge and the other drone was to scout around, and both were to transmit their live video as they flew.

I went into the living room of the Family Flyer to monitor the split screen video images on the large screen TV.

What the children were saying was correct, as we could see the Boomerang Beast dressed in his fearsome suit, first destroying the bridge with an axe, and then pouring fuel all over the bridge.

Kat, who had now joined me with some of the children gazed at the screen and then at me with a very puzzled face.

"What's he doing?", Kat said, worryingly.

"What's happening.

It's the middle of the night," said a sleep ridden Skye as she entered the living room, rubbing the sleep from her eyes.

BB destroying the Bridge & Catching Fire.

Kat suggested, "Did we do this to him, Jack – asking him to come back with us.

Asking Jimi Jack to leave his friends and his home for the last three years."

"Maybe he just can't bear to leave Matilda behind, tomorrow, and now he's just gone into one", Skye piped in.

The video images on the screen now showed that the Boomerang Beast was smashing the handrails of the new bridge with a large axe, and pouring fuel on to the walkway and was about to set light to it, but then something went very wrong.

After he bent down to light the fuel, a quick flame travelled along the glistening gas to the can, where it exploded in a huge fireball with an enormous bang, setting the Boomerang Beast on fire.

He started shouting and spinning around erratically, all to no avail, and decided an instant later, to plunge into the toxic river to put out the flaming protective suit.

Meanwhile, Kat, Skye and I were distraught to see what was unfolding in front of our eyes on the video screen.

"Oh my god – Jimi Jack", Kat cried.

We could see that our son was now sinking in the river and drowning.

I set "Triple One" to assist remotely, by fishing around underwater with its long, telescoping arms.

Suddenly it struck lucky and grabbed on to a hand and pulled the Boomerang Beast to the surface.

Next, an arm broke through the surface of the water as he managed to gulp in some air, after which, he swam a few strokes until he reached the edge, before crawling on to the muddy bank.

Amy wearing BB's Suit.

Two decomposing skeletons appeared to look on gleefully, as if to say, "Ha, Ha, we nearly got you.

You will soon be joining us."

Then the Boomerang Beast slumped face down and lay motionless, in the mud.

Was he dead, unconscious or just resting - but why did he want to destroy the new bridge?

The second drone, triple 2, was now displaying its video image on another part of the large living room monitor.

It was circling Matilda's caravan in the orchard and as it did, Matilda came to the open door, having just been awoken from her sleep by the buzzing drone and she looked up straight at the drone for a moment.

"What's going on", Jimi Jack said quietly, to Mati, coming up behind her to give her a kiss on the back of her neck.
He had also just woken up.

We all watched the new intriguing, but confusing, video images on the screen and I said, "Wait, if Jimi Jack is with Mati, then who's dressed in his suit and just destroyed the bridge?"

Skye said, "Yeah, who's on the riverbank, right now, burned and half drowned?"

On the bank of the river, the helmet of the Boomerang Beast's suit was being removed, revealing it was Amy, one of Mati's older girls.

She turned over on to her back and faced looking up towards the night sky, "Triple One", hovered around her and zoomed into her face.

Amy being helped from the river.

Luckily, she had the Boomerang Beast's protective suit on but why did she do this?

Everyone was wondering and thankfully, Jimi Jack was safe and well with Mati in her caravan.

"Triple One," was now showing that some of the other children had caught up with Amy as she collected the Boomerang Beast's helmet from the mud and took a few steps out of the poisonous water on to dry land to meet the others.

Both drones still transmitted pictures to the screen in the Family Flyer living room for us to view.

Meanwhile we were thinking that Amy was lucky to still be alive after first, being engulfed by flames and then nearly drowning in the poisonous water.

Will she be alright tonight?

Has the radioactive water affected her?

Will it make her sick by morning or in the future?

Kat suggested that Amy had always had a crush on Jimi Jack and her jealously got the better of her when Mati and our son became an item.

Amy wanted to punish the Boomerang Beast by framing him and making it look as if he was destroying the bridge.

Maybe she was simply upset that he was possibly leaving and by destroying the bridge he might stay behind to rebuild it.

Skye suggested that Amy lost her family in the early days when the bombs hit, and could not stand to see a loving family searching for their son, finding him and taking him back with them.

I thought it might be a mixture of all these reasons and that Amy had some mental health issues to deal with.

I was just glad to go back to bed, happy that the drama was all over, and that no one was seriously hurt.

Jimi Jack Cleaning the microphone.

Chapter 005—Jimi Jack's Dream.

That night Jimi Jack—the Boomerang Beast, had a dream where he was dressed in overalls with the words "SOUND CREW" printed on his back.

He was on stage where he began to set up a microphone.

He placed it in the holder and tested it tapping it a few times he says, "One, two, three four, testing, testing".

He then unhooked a spray cleaner from his waist and sprayed the gleaming chrome microphone stand to clear any marks or fingerprints from it.

As he did this he began humming a tune. It was the song, "I can't help falling in love with you", made famous by Elvis Presley.

After cleaning and humming for a few moments, he begins singing the words not realizing that his voice was being amplified around a huge football stadium and crowds of people were starting to notice.

Some were turning around to see what was going on - who was singing and why?

The Boomerang Beast's song continued...

"Wise men say only fools rush in but I can't help falling in love with you".

A television camera zoomed in to a close-up of his face and displayed it on the giant video screen behind BB but he was still unaware of this and some of the crowd began to join in with him while he sang his song and as he continued to clean the lower parts of the microphone stand.

Mati talking to 3J's on phones.

After a few more seconds BB got to the part of the song with the words...

"Like a river flows downwards to the sea, darling, you and me we're always just meant to be."

Jimi Jack did not realize that by now the whole stadium crowd is singing along with him with some people swaying left to right in time to the music.

His phone rang and he answered the call to Matilda.

She said, "Jimi what's going on - you are singing—the microphone is amplifying your voice - the whole audience can hear and see you on the giant video screen."

BB answered, "Oh, I'm sorry I didn't mean anything bad by it...where are you... come on out here on to the field."

The audience in the stadium had just heard his phone conversation, they stopped singing and were now intrigued to see what was going to happen next.

Mati walked out on to the lush green football field and the camera followed her showing her walking while she is displayed on the giant video screen.

Jimi Jack begins to remove his outer overalls revealing he is wearing his Boomerang Beast, armored protective suit but without his helmet.

Mati walked up close to him and when she was at arms distance from him, he knelt down on one knee.

The Boomerang Beast Proposes to Mati.

Matilda brought a hand up to her mouth in disbelief.

The vast, football stadium audience gasped and said, "Oh".

Everyone seemed overjoyed.

Jimi stood up and talked directly into the microphone in a very matter of fact way and said, "Oh, I forgot something - I need a ring".

At that very moment a large UFO with pulsating lights appeared and then hovered motionless over the stadium absolutely silently.

A second or two later an intense beam of light hit the ground a few paces from Jimi Jack, and from this beam a tall grey alien emerged and handed Jimi Jack a small red box.

A close-up on the giant screen showed that it was a beautiful and precious, diamond and gold, engagement ring.

Jimi said, "Thank you," to the alien who then stood beside him and the crowd gasped in amazement while Jimi Jack settled back down on to one knee.

Matilda, by now, is stood right in front of Jimi as he said,

"You are my best friend and I love you more than anything in the world. Will you marry me".

The large stadium crowd erupted in huge whoops and applause.

Matilda nodded profusely saying repeatedly, "Yes, yes, yes of course".

Jimi stood up and kissed his girlfriend and suddenly the stadium is silent and empty.

Matilda is suddenly wearing Kathleen's, wedding dress as the alien stepped back into his beam of light and disappeared up into his UFO, which in turn disappeared at an impossible speed back into the sky.

3J's bewildered by the two females.

Jimi waved as he watched the space ship disappear and when he turned back to Matilda, it was not her in the wedding dress any longer, but his sister, Skye".

Mati and Skye changed back and forwards repeatedly confusing Jimi Jack, the Boomerang Beast.

He reached out to the changing female figures, their faces changing, in the wedding dress, as he called out in disbelief, "No, no, no, no".

Jimi Jack opened his eyes, now awake and quite bewildered by his dream.

"Whatever could this dream mean?"

Back in reality and the next morning, Kat and I woke up to a beautiful blue sunny day.

Skye was cleaning the glass of the Family Flyer, and Kathleen and I were packing away the camping equipment in silence.

I guess we were thinking what an anti-climax it was to have lost our son, only to have found him after three years, and then to have lost him again.

I was going to leave him a couple of cell phone handsets and also a radio, so at least we could be in communication with him and the two clans from now on, but it would not be the same as having our son come with us.

Nearly ready for departure from the Orchard.

Just about the time we had packed everything away and we were ready to set off, Jimi Jack and Matilda emerged from the woods and into the clearing where the Family Flyer stood ready for take-off.

At first glance I thought it was good that Jimi Jack and Matilda came to say goodbye, but then I noticed he was carrying a hold-all in one of his hands, with his fearsome Boomerang Beast outfit and his boomerangs all packed away.

Instead, he was wearing one of our Family Flyer flight suits and carried a large backpack in one hand.

Kat and I looked at one another in disbelief.

"You got room for one more, Dad—Mum?" Jimi Jack asked in a quiet voice.

Kat's huge smile said it all.

She mimed the words, "Thank you," to Matilda, and Matilda acknowledged Kathleen's appreciation with an extra-large beaming smile and a nod.

We each hugged Matilda for a moment, and I patted Jimi Jack and said, "Should we get going then?"

I handed over the cell-phones and radio to Mati and a minute or two later we were hundreds of feet above the clearing, waving goodbye to our friends below, watching the campsite, the poisoned river and the apple orchard disappear into the misty morning haze.

"That Way".

"This is some nice machine you got here, Dad", the still unfamiliar voice said from the seat directly behind me.

"Welcome aboard the Family Flyer, son," I replied.

"Hear, hear," we all heard over the airplanes communication system.

It was truly a moment of joy for us all, but I did wonder what Matilda had said to convince the fearsome Boomerang Beast to leave his clan, the responsibilities of a leader and his home for the last three years, and more importantly, to leave his newly found love, all behind.

"I guess I will just have to save that conversation for another day and when I've got to know my son a little better," I thought to myself.

"Mum, Dad, where to?", Skye said, over the airplane's communication system.

I took a moment to look out of the tinted windows at the huge expanse of golden, barren, desert, two thousand feet below, and pointed randomly inland, and answered,

"That way."

The Care home Living Room.

CHAPTER 006 - The Care home.

Using his walking frame, Bernard David Collins shuffled over to the window, as he did every day, and carefully, looking over his shoulder, he lowered himself into his favourite arm chair.

Bernie, as he was known, made a point of having his tea and biscuits each day at the same time while looking out of the window, just in case something happened outside.

In actual fact nothing had happened recently, and not since the occupants of the residential home emerged from the basement underground car park nearly a year ago.

Two men had died of old age, and one of them of chemical contamination after he ate a plum from a tree in the garden.

It was Arthur's own fault, because the residents were told time and time again not to do that, but like a naughty boy he snuck out one evening and ate the plum.

This made him so ill and, being eighty-five, like Bernie, he did not have the strength to fight the contamination.

Nina and Tina, the carers of the Azouri Care Home, made tea three times a day for the few remaining residents who were more than happy living above ground, since the air had become breathable and the radiation levels were mostly back to normal.

The Old hospital, a few blocks away, was one of the first places targeted by the bombers, using dirty bombs, which left many dead and injured, and most of the survivors soon died of the lingering radiation or the deadly pink mist which followed.

Bernie spots the Family Flyer.

Bernie lost everybody he knew to this ridiculous war.

He hated aggression of all kinds.

He even thought that arguing with others was a waste of time and energy.

He was truly a pacifist, quick to smile, and such a lovely caring man.

A couple of sips of his tea and a mouthful of digestive biscuit later, and he was up like a shot from his chair.

He spotted a white dot moving across the bright blue sky.

Bernie put down his cup and saucer so quickly that it spilled everywhere but he was going to just ignore it.

He munched and swallowed his digestive biscuit so fast that it made him cough while Nina could do no more than watch Bernie.

"Look, look, something is up there.

Look it's flying.

It's up there in the sky", Bernie shouted excitedly, spluttering tea and biscuit everywhere.

Of course, he did not know it yet, and nor did we, but he was looking at us in the Family Flyer, four thousand feet up and twelve miles away.

He staggered out onto the street outside the Care Home, moving faster than he had in many months, and set his readymade bonfire alight with a lighter that he always kept in his pocket.

By the door he always kept a dry stick and a can of gasoline - just in case.

Within two minutes, the newspaper, old chairs and book shelf, cushions, twigs, old boots and clothes, erupted into a spectacular blaze of bluish, grey, smoke, which rose quickly into the sky, much to the amazement and worry of the carers and the other residents.

Bernie's Bonfire.

Bernie and some of the elderly folks were all coughing from the smoke while one old man was shouting "I'm an aeroplane," and another old woman was calling, "Fire, Fire", and running around in small circles, waving her arms around hysterically.

It was actually Kathleen who spotted the straight vertical line of smoke in the distance from the cockpit of the Family Flyer.

"Guys, over there," she said in a matter-of-fact manner.

Without a moment of hesitation Skye banked the Family Flyer left, towards the bluish grey plume of smoke.

Our sudden manoeuvre made Bernie and the elderly residents even more excited, as they could see that the dot was now headed straight towards them, getting closer by the second, and the dot was actually an aeroplane, the first aircraft anyone had seen in years— and what a strange looking aeroplane it was.

We circled around the excited group for a few moments, who were by now moving erratically around Bernie's bonfire like disturbed ants.

We waved through the canopy of the cockpit at them for a moment, and then headed for a landing place just down the street to where they were positioned.

Moments later we were shaking hands with Bernie, the other elderly residents and their careers, Nina and Tina.

They explained how over the weeks leading up to the bombs, they had the good sense to move down to the two underground basement floors, stock up on medication, food, water and even some DVD and Blu-ray movies.

I told them of our own struggles, of losing our son and then the joy of finding him again.

We talked about the aeroplane and how we met the children of the two warring clans, and the people at the university, and setting Banshee up at the radio station and how wonderful it was to see these elderly folks so alive and well.

Testing toxicity levels.

I congratulated Bernie on his organisational skills regarding the bonfire, and being so observant, spotting us in the sky and asked if there was anything we could do for them.

As it turned out, there was quite a lot we could do for the residents and the carers of the Azouri care home.

Skye and Kat began bringing furniture up above ground, decorating the communal lounge, and making the place more homely and habitable again, while Jimi Jack and I took a short flight over to the Old Hospital just a mile or so down the road.

It was our intention to bring back some good articulated beds for those folks who found it hard to get in and out of bed, and to bring back some wheelchairs and heart monitoring equipment, but as soon as we touched down on the street in front of the hospital our sensors read high levels of radiation.

Wearing our masks, we disembarked the Family Flyer and headed for the foyer.

It was locked with a large, rusty padlock and chain, which gave way quite easily, and we continued on inside the dusty, dilapidated building.

We soon reached the top floor where we could see in the harsh shadows, broken medical containers, and hurriedly abandoned side cabinets that had toppled over onto the grit and rubble, laden floor.

Our sensors showed high levels of toxic gas in the desolate wards, but an almost safe level of radiation.

I said, "Jimi Jack, open all the windows.

Let's get some air and light in here."

3J's didn't even try to open the windows the conventional way.

He simply used a heavy, rusting wheelchair and threw it through the nearest glass window, for ventilation.

Before long the toxicity levels showed it was safe to breathe the air without our gasmasks on, in a few of the old wards.

The abandoned wards.

Another sensor started flashing on my display, which showed a higher than usual, carbon dioxide level, so I started preparing myself subconsciously for other people to be around, but I was not prepared for what followed next - not prepared at all.

I could vaguely make out two green skinned figures, standing motionless at the end of a long dark corridor.

I pointed them out to Jimi Jack but before he could see them, they scurried off, quick as a flash.

"Jimi, Jack," I said quietly into the intercom.

"We have company, so watch yourself."

I could hear movement in the ceiling, in the walls, and in the air conditioning ducts. Jimi Jack was investigating a large storeroom and said, "We've hit the jackpot here, Dad.

"There's masses of bandages and Penicillin, Antibiotics, other kinds of medicine, and loads more besides,

"3J's continued.

"That's great, I'll be right along".

Most interestingly, I was mulling over the fact that Jimi Jack had just called me Dad, and I had not heard him do that for over three years.

It was a heart-warming feeling, which made me smile to myself.

This warm feeling was broken by a scream from my son in my earpiece.

"Argghh, Dad, they've stabbed me," he yelped into my headset.

I quickly made my way from one of the abandoned wards, trying not to slip on the grit on the floors, and entered the storeroom to find Jimi Jack getting up off the floor, bleeding from the shoulder with a bloodied piece of wood, sticking out of him.

"They just dropped out of the ceiling and attacked me for no reason, Dad," he said in a surprised and angry voice.

I took a close look at his shoulder and said, "Lucky it's just a flesh wound, Son. An inch either way and it could have been a lot worse".

We heard further movement above our heads while I pulled the pointed stick out of Jimi Jack's shoulder, and then we heard the storeroom door lock from the outside with a loud click.

Escaping the Hospital store fire.

I sterilised and dressed his wound using the medicine and bandages around us and noticed some flames and smoke entering the storeroom from the gap under the door.

"They're trying to smoke us out, Dad," Jimi Jack said, nervously.

"Put your mask on." I suggested, to my son as I started looking around for a way out.

Suddenly I heard the sound of glass breaking against the outside of the storeroom door, which was followed by a small explosion.

A large fire immediately engulfed both sides of the storeroom door.

Jimi Jack and I looked at each other in disbelief as this situation was becoming more serious and worse by the second.

I tried not to panic and said calmly, "Let's try to get this window open."

At the rear of the storeroom was a large window, but it had a security grill screwed to the wall in several places, in front of it.

"But it's four storeys high, Dad," Jimi Jack said through his gasmask.

"Don't worry, I've got a plan. You just try and get this grill off," I said, while the lethal smoke was quickly filling the small storeroom.

In the two minutes that followed, Jimi Jack and I, using all our might, ripped the grill from the wall, and I also, I remotely controlled the Family Flyer, parked down at street level, via my iPhone, to take off and circle around the building and then to hover besides, the now open window.

I remotely lowered the cockpit door stairs and we carefully stepped onto the aircraft, one at a time, a hundred feet or so off the ground.

First Jimi Jack stepped gingerly on, and then myself, the stability sensors compensating for each wobble that our steps made.

I quickly took my seat in the cockpit, at the front of the aeroplane, touched the "Rise up slowly", button on the iPhone touch screen, which controlled the Family Flyer, to head upwards and away from the burning building.

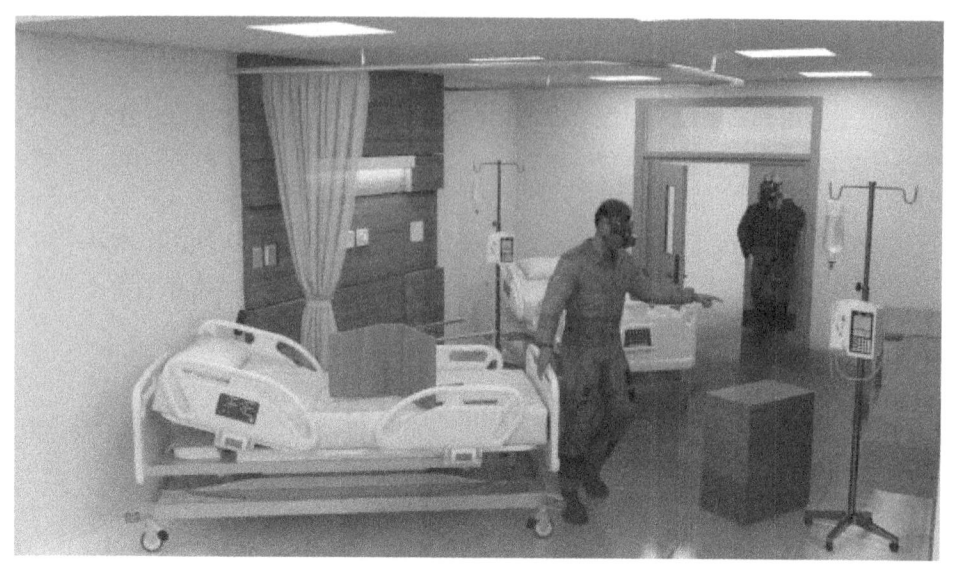

The newer wards.

We could now clearly see a half dozen or so, goblin-like creatures, on the roof, along with rusting beds and old mattresses.

By now the storeroom was fully ablaze, with the occasional explosion caused by bottles of alcohol and other flammable liquids.

From circling around outside, we could see more green skinned figures putting the fire out with hand-held extinguishers and buckets of water, until the thick black smoke changed to white, and then became no more than a gentle flame with a small amount of smoke.

From time to time more green skinned people would come to the window to watch us hovering around the building.

They shouted and made arm waving gestures and shook their fists toward us.

I guess they were trying to say, "Stay away, this is our place", even though it was clear to me that they didn't use the wards or ever access the storerooms.

Maybe they, like many others, lived in the depths of the hospital, to try and survive the horrors of the last few years. Two days later Jimi Jack and I went back to the Old Hospital, but this time we came bearing gifts of a basket of apples and plastic containers of cider.

We landed on the street briefly, unloaded quickly and took off leaving the gifts.

After a few moments the green people appeared and checked the basket of apples and the cider for radiation and contamination, and after vigorous nodding to each other, began munching on the apples and swigging back the cider, before running off with our gifts.

We landed on the street a little later and entered the hospital at ground floor level for further exploration while the green people had disappeared, altogether.

The next day we did a similar thing.

We landed as usual, put another basket of apples and some cider just outside the Family Flyer but this time we stayed locked in the aeroplane until the green people came around to collect the gifts.

Once they had run off with the apples and cider we thought it might be safe enough to go back into the hospital to take another look around for equipment and medicines for the elderly folk at the care home.

This time we went further into the newer parts of the hospital where we found working remote controlled electric beds and other untouched store rooms filled with clean, boxed medicines.

Airlifting beds and equipment.

The green people kept watch on us all the while but, thankfully, they kept their distance.

Our strategy was working - they were beginning to think that we were not a threat to them at all.

This gave us a chance to select a half dozen articulated hospital beds, a couple of motorized wheelchairs, monitoring equipment and other useful equipment.

Finally, we carried everything out that we wanted, to the Family Flyer, prepared a mixture of anti-bacterial-anti radioactive solution and thoroughly drenched each item.

We loaded what we could into the back space of the airplane, which was also Kat and my, bedroom, having folded the double bed up against the wall to make space.

Then 3J's and I strung as much together as we could with rope and air lifted everything back to the old folks in a couple of trips.

Each time we landed the green people would do the same thing.

They would begin shouting and gesturing then run off with the basket of apples and cider which we left for them and then they would leave us alone for a while to gather whatever we wanted from the hospital.

Once we brought everything back to the residential home, Kat and Skye took over giving the beds, furniture and equipment a final clean, before wheeling the items off to individual bedrooms and the various locations around the residential home.

Bernie was overjoyed to see his remote-controlled bed.

He lay down on the waterbed mattress and pushed some buttons.

The bed inflated, deflated, went up then down, before finally tilting sideways to let him off the bed a lot easier.

I guess when you are young and healthy you take your mobility for granted, but Bernie shook my hand, hugged us all, and thanked the family for everything we had done.

He was very concerned with Jimi Jacks' stabbed shoulder but 3J's said was OK and it was not a problem.

Dinner at the Care home.

I left Bernie and the carers with a cell phone and a radio, and spent a few moments showing them how to use them.

We had a short discussion about the few pockets of people that could now all talk to each other, and Bernie said he would spend time contacting them.

We all agreed there was still danger lurking at the Old Hospital a few blocks away, and maybe we needed to try to pool together and try to either flush the green people out, or try to come to some agreement where we could all live in peace.

After a beautiful dinner of fresh pasta and Bolognese sauce with real beef and Italian oregano spices, we drank orange and mango, fruit juice, finishing with ice cream and chocolate sauce.

I had forgotten that just a few weeks before we were calculating our food, water and calorie intake so carefully.

In that moment it almost seemed that it just might be possible for mankind to be peaceful, normal and civilised once again.

Only now we had strange, deformed creatures with green skins to worry about, just down the road.

We said our final goodbyes to Bernie, the residents and the staff of the residential home, and thanked them for such a lovely meal, before all the family clambered aboard the Flyer.

Watching them through the canopy I felt sad we were leaving, but I brushed that thought aside and said, "Skye, honey, take us home."

She said, "Really - home - Freedom Point - home?"

I nodded and just smiled at her.

Dropping 3J's off in the carpark.

CHAPTER 7 -
Back To Freedom Point.

Four hours and twenty-seven minutes later we could see in the distance, the mountain, which our home was built onto.

With the powerful nose camera of the aircraft, I zoomed in to see a lime green graffiti logo sprawled across the concrete gantry viewing deck wall, at the car park level, at the base of Freedom Point.

The car park was strewn with cardboard boxes and general discarded garbage and just for a second, I thought I caught a glimpse of a woman with her head covered, in dark clothes, carrying a child.

There was smoke rising into the air from a smouldering bonfire and two Landover vehicles, were haphazardly, parked amongst the moss, the puddles and the greenery growing through the cracks, of the carpark's surface.

We had been invaded by people venturing out of the cities now that the radiation and air toxicity levels were nearly back to normal?

We landed the Family Flyer in the carpark, and Skye dropped 3J's and myself off by the entrance, and near the remnants of the bonfire.

I walked up the grassy ramp to the solid concrete door pulling on a small, concealed flap hidden into the hillside and placed my palm squarely on the reader to open the door.

Meanwhile, Skye flew Kat up in the Family Flyer to the house level and landed on the small runway just outside the front door.

The luminant green graffiti was now clear for me to see.

The simple circular logo of a sad sun with a downturned mouth, sunrays all around and spots for eyes, did the trick to worry me.

It was the logo of the misguided Sad Sun Eco terrorist group responsible for much of the killing and devastation brought to our world in the name of saving the planet from humanity, and now some of them were right here trying to gain entrance to our property and our home.

Walking through the vehicle tunnel.

Jimi Jack said, "The fire's still smouldering and the car door is open so they must have left in a hurry when they saw us arriving. They can't be too far away".

I said, "Watch your back. They have been here for a while but I don't think they have managed to get in to any hangers or the house".

The concrete bunker doors opened noiselessly. A small one, at the viewing gantry level, where I stood, and the main doors just below, to let Jimi Jack in.

The corridor lights came on automatically and flickered for a moment revealing a damp underground vehicle tunnel which led to the lift, museum and the house a few floors above.

It was just a short walk through the aircraft equipment and parked vehicles, we hurriedly stored away around when the bombs went off, and I was satisfied that no one had broken in as there was no paint, footprints or any sign of anyone entering the tunnel.

We shot up a few floors in the lift past the Tourist reception floor, and continued up to the top-most level of our house.

I could see Jimi Jack looking quite unsettled as he took in the familiar, but nearly forgotten views of the place he lived, worked and loved, a few years earlier.

We exited the lift and stepped on to the tarmac of the short runway where the Family Flyer was now parked.

The huge concrete dome still protecting our home inside it, as we had left it months earlier. I activated the "Open Dome" button on the iPad and the huge half-sphere began to reveal the house and pool which had safely nestled under it.

We all smiled and gasped a sigh of relief as the house lights activated and the protective dome came to a standstill.

We entered our house with warm and happy feelings and soon we were in the familiar surroundings of the living room, kitchen and adjoining bedrooms.

"Wow, Dad, you've done a lot to this place while I've been away," Jimi Jack said. I smiled and put my arm around his shoulders and said, "Nice to have you home, son. You can remember where your bedroom is, can't you?". Jimi Jack nodded and headed away looking very content, and he was by no means, the only one.

I was looking forward to a bit of normality in our own home without the daily drama we had encountered for the last few months.

As Jimi Jack lay on his comfortable bed, tears welling in his eyes, he remembered what happened on the day all this started…

3J's boarding the bus.

Chapter 008 -
Jimi Jack's Journey.

The shuttle bus arrived in the lower car park at Freedom Point, really early - four thirty A.M. and the sun was just rising.

I was the last one of the students to be collected and Mr Hook, my Physical Education Teacher, called me on my phone to tell me they were downstairs and waiting for me.

We were setting off for a week away at camp.

It was to be about learning new bush craft skills and experiencing a taste of personal independence.

It was going to be rough and rugged - Oh, and that reminded me - I had better take my headphones so I could make this a more bearable trip.

I had already downloaded my favourite songs and apps the night before.

I was dreading not having Wi Fi and sleeping in an unfamiliar bed for the week, but at least Dave and Russell were going to be there and of course, Amanda.

I hugged Mum and Dad in the house and set off downstairs with my bag.

We already agreed that they were not going to come down to the bus to embarrass me by hugging and kissing me in front of all the other kids.

After all I was grown up now and sixteen and nearly a man.

The shuttle bus doors unfolded open with a hiss and Dave and Russell called out in unison, "Here he is".

Mr Hook said, "Mornin', Jimi Jack.

Take a seat and buckle up.

We've got a long drive ahead".

The others nodded a hello, as I stepped on to the bus, but some were asleep or had their headphones on.

Amanda glanced up from her phone for a moment and smiled a small controlled smile in my direction and honestly, that was more than enough for me at that moment.

Watching the mushroom cloud.

Mr Hook sat up front, where he could chat to the female driver, Miss Carter, who was also a PE teacher, coming on the trip.

I sat with my friends and before long we were exiting the road from Freedom Point and rounding Sloping Bridge Curve, to join the main, busy, highway which skirted around the city.

It felt like we were on the bus for days but it was actually only about four hours before we were on a quiet desert highway, several miles away from the city when suddenly, we all experienced an extremely bright light coming from the right side of the bus and from the other side of the mountains.

This was followed by a loud "Boom" and the ground started shaking quite dramatically.

Mr Hook shouted out, "Hold on everyone - it's an earthquake".

I thought, "Earthquakes don't give out light and it can't be a thunder storm either, as there were no rain clouds in the sky".

The moving ground bounced the bus up and down, shaking us all like rag dolls for a few moments and if it was not for the insistence of Mr Hook making us all wear our seatbelts, many of us would have been seriously injured.

The bus continued on, best it could, and we watched the ground and the road in front of us undulating like waves on an ocean.

A few minutes later and the dust, literally, settled when the bus came to a halt at the side of the desert highway.

We all quickly disembarked the shuttle bus amidst a hot, dusty, sand storm, which whistled furiously around us, while a huge fiery, white, mushroom cloud rose high into the blue and white sky, many miles away, where the city stood.

It was a nuclear explosion which was beautiful and very frighting, both, at the same time.

Mr Hooks' short speech.

Mr Hook made us board the bus quickly, and after a few minutes of trying to use his phone and some discussion with Miss Carter at the front of the bus, he turned to us all and said, "Listen guys, I think something serious has happened.

That was no earthquake just then.

It's obvious that the city has been attacked and I think the best thing is that we continue on to Camp.

At least it's away from the city and we should be safe there.

I can't get a signal on my phone but as soon as I do I will let you know more.

Keep your eyes peeled and let Miss Carter and I know if you see anything out of the ordinary."

We all sat in stunned silence after listening to Mr Hook's short speech, as the bus continued on down the desert highway.

Everyone on the bus tried their phones without success as I thought about Mum, Dad and Skye at home.

At least they were far away from the city just like we were, and furthermore, they had the protective dome they could use to cover the house.

Of course I did not know it then, but that was exactly what they did back at Freedom Point.

Right now I had to concentrate on the problem at hand.

Were we all going to be safe?

Who was attacking the city and why?

How far was the camp?

My thoughts were soon interrupted….
"Sir, Sir, Sir - There is some kind of roadblock up ahead," Russell and Dave called out in unison, to the pair of PE teachers up front.

Many of us stood up to get a better view and then we could see it.

Stretched fully across the road, was a metal fence supported by huge blocks of concrete and some make-shift road signs saying the road ahead was closed.

A black Hummer was parked just beyond the fence but also, high up on a hill to the right of us, was another dark vehicle.

Outside the bus.

Some soldiers emerged, carrying rifles and wearing dark uniforms, as the bus approached the roadblock.

Now it was clear to see.

The soldiers waved us down to stop the bus.

They were wearing dark helmets with dark visors and dark masks.

Their helmets and breast plates showed the bright yellow logo of the Sad Sun Environmental group, a sad looking emoji with sun rays all around.

The soldier in charge kicked at the door for Miss Carter to let him in.

He, and another soldier boarded the bus and walked up and down the aisle looking at all of us very intently, and then without a word, the soldier gestured with his rifle, for all of us to get off the bus.

"Excuse me, but what is going on.

We are just a school going on a science field trip to camp", Mr Hook started to say, but the soldier in charge was not interested.

Instead, he slammed the butt of his rifle into Mr Hook's face and roared like an angry lion, and then he pointed his rifle hard up against Mr Hook's temple and gestured once again for all of us to get off the bus.

"OK, OK, you want us all to get off the bus", Mr Hook said, a little bit dazed and raising his arms up in submission, and confirming what the soldiers wanted us to do.

Mr Hook, continued, "Come on guys, don't be afraid.

Quickly and quietly let's do what they want and get off the bus".

It was only a minute or two before we were all standing outside in the hazy, dusty, desert heat, and off the bus, with our hands up, when the Sad Sun Soldiers started making strange sounds like they were being punched, and dropping to the ground, their arms, limbs and torsos, exploding bursts of blood in all directions.

They were being shot from a long way away but we could not hear the sound of any gun fire, just the bullets hitting their mark like fearsome punches.

The new soldiers arrive.

"Thud, thud", and another Sad Sun soldier went down.

They did not even call out or groan.

They just fell to the ground in silence.

"Everyone get down, someone is shooting", Miss Carter screamed, as we all dropped to the ground instantly.

I could see clearly that the soldiers, now lying in the dirt, had been shot as they were bleeding enormous pools of dark red blood and one was hurriedly, limping along, trying to get to the protection of the Hummer just on the other side of the roadblock fence.

"Thud, thud", and he was shot down, also.

The Sad Sun soldiers fired back aimlessly shooting at shadows, at the distant trees and hills but there was no one there to shoot at.

Suddenly a fast-moving armoured vehicle, with soldiers in futuristic black and white battle protection suits, carrying guns, came over one of the nearby hills.

"Everybody, stay down and do not move", their leader belted out.

I lifted my head to see who was now shouting orders at us but he just screamed at me.

"You, keep your head down or you might get it shot off."

I quickly dropped my head down onto the hot, prickly, tarmac and sand covered road.

"They're just a school party, Sarge", one of the new soldiers called to their leader.

I soon realised there were four of these new soldiers who were scurrying amongst us and kneeling down occasionally, to check if the Sad Sun soldiers were breathing or not.

Examining a Sad Sun soldier.

"All clear, Sarge", another soldier shouted out, when suddenly there was a burst of machine gun fire and the new soldier was shot by a Sad Sun soldier.

A second later and the Sarge shot the Sad Sun soldier dead.

"Lewis, Lewis how bad is it, the Sarge said to the new soldier who had just been shot.

"Sorry Sarge, it's my leg, he got my leg, I can't walk - I thought he was...."

It's OK Lewis, it's not your fault, it's hard to tell with these guys, as they're MM's, Manufactured Mortals – clones - they don't even talk - can't tell sometimes, if they're breathing or not.

Let's fix Lewis's leg up and get him on the bus with you and we will escort you to your camp, the Sargent said.

"Come on, you all need to get back on to the bus right now", the Sarge continued, with a sense of urgency, to us all.
"We've been patrolling this area all week as we knew that some Sad Sun bandits were attacking people along this road for the last couple of days and you guys are lucky to still be alive", the Sarge said.

"Thanks to you," I said, dusting myself down and addressing the leader of the new soldiers.

The Sargent, who was known to his men as Sarge, explained that the city had been attacked with a small nuclear device as many cities around the world had been, today.

"Let's get you guys to the safety of your camp.

I hope you don't mind taking Lewis with you on the bus.

Attack of the bus.

He will be more comfortable", the Sarge asked the PE teachers, politely.

"Yes, that's fine Miss Carter and Mr Hook both replied, in unison.

Not long afterwards we all helped to clear the roadblock items.

We tucked the Sad Sun soldiers' bodies out of the sun, under some bushes, but before that the Sarge showed us the face of one of them.

The MM had no mouth or teeth or ears - just small holes where his ears should have been.

We then set off again on the bus, following our new friends and protectors, towards the camp.

Lewis removed his super soldier, armoured suit outfit and helmet, revealing he had been shot just above the knee.

We stopped the bleeding best we could and washed off the blood with some bottles of water.

All the while we followed the new soldiers armoured truck, which towed a small covered, trailer.

Lewis said, "Keep your eyes peeled for more of the bandits and the pink mist.

Oh, and especially their killer drones.

They are particularly nasty."

"Pink mist, killer drones, cloned human bandits, what had we got ourselves into", I thought.

It was all very quiet on the bus for the next hour or so and it was also becoming dark, when we finally drove up the road which would take us into the camp.

What a day it had been since I left Freedom Point early this morning.

A city had been destroyed, we had been threatened with guns in our faces, saved by some super soldiers, and a bunch of manufactured, humanoid bandits were killed.

What's next, I wondered?

I did not have to wait long to know the answer to that question....

3J's aims the RPG.

From out of nowhere we were being fired upon by two menacing, angular, shapes in the darkening sky.

The armoured vehicle, in front of us was being machine gunned by a dark, hovering drone with bright, white lights.

They too had the yellow, Sad Sun logo's, painted on their hulls.

The Sarge, was swerving from left to right trying to avoid being hit by fiery lines of bullets, while the soldiers on the back were shooting up at the drones.

The second drone was now targeting our bus.

Bullets were ripping through the front windscreen and I could see Miss Carter and Mr Hook being hit and falling over.

The ceiling of the bus was being ripped apart, windows were being shattered, bullets were hitting seats and our bags, causing small fires to erupt here and there.

Mr Hook was motionless on the floor of the bus while Miss Carter was now slumped over the steering wheel which made the bus pull off the dirt road, straight into a dense clump of trees, where we managed to gain some cover, away from the pair of dangerous Sad Sun, Drones.

The remainder of us did our best to get off the bus as fast as we could, climbing out of the shattered windows and headed deeper, into the trees.

The bus was now on its side and on fire in several places.

The two evil drones manoeuvred around the bus and came in for another attack firing their guns, hitting Dave and Russell in their backs as they ran towards the trees.

They fell to the ground in heaps.

Lewis, loaded his Rocket Propelled Grenade launcher, blood pouring from his temple and said, "I'm a gonna.

It's up to you, mate.

Aim and pull the trigger", he said, handing me his weapon with his dyeing breath.

The two drones came in for a final attack, blue flames gushing from their engines and blasting machine gun fire at the bus and towards me.

The Sarge brings out the suit.

I did what Lewis, instructed.

I took aim and fired, and with a loud "WOOSH" the RPG streaked off, towards one of the drones which caused it to explode and spiral down to the ground and explode for a second time.

The second drone was already on the ground, hit by another RPG fired by the Sarge from his vehicle and that too, exploded, fell to the ground, and exploded again.

Suddenly, it was very quiet.

I could just hear the crackling of parts of the bus on fire.

I was heartbroken to see Amanda lying on the ground a few metres away, her pink skirt stained with blood and her legs sticking out from just behind a tree.

"I am so sorry, Jimi Jack".

She's gone and all the others too.
There's just you and me now.

Let's get ourselves together and get the hell out of here before more evil drones and Sad Sun bandits come back to finish us off".

A pink mist was moving slowly down the hills towards us and the Sarge's armoured vehicle was now fully ablaze.

The Sarge emerged from the partially, burning bus with Lewis's protective suit and said," Put this on.

It will give you some protection against the pink mist".

The mist might look pretty but it's basically, poisonous, radioactive gas and should be avoided at all costs - if you don't want it to melt your brain".

I was totally in shock and I just nodded.

I felt like I was in some horrific, virtual reality, war game, so I followed the Sarge's instructions, and as quickly as I could, I put Lewis's protective suit on and began to follow the Sarge, a few steps behind, into the woods, on foot.

We could see the camp down below in the valley and it was teaming with Sad Sun bandits and evil drones buzzing around in all directions.

The club house wall.

The Sarge did not have to say anything, as I knew what his look meant.

There was no way the camp was going to be a safe place for us to shelter any more.

In fact, it was just the opposite.

It would be certain capture or even death, if we entered the camp.

I whispered quietly into the small microphone in my helmet.

"I'm going to kill every one of those Sad Sun bandits.

Destroy every one of those evil drones.

I'm going to rip them to shreds like they did to my friends.

I'm...I'm..." I smashed my fist down on my knee and felt my blood pump loudly at my temples and in my ears.

I could feel such rage in me, such sadness, such pain like I had never felt in my life before - I just wanted justice and more importantly, I wanted revenge.

The Sarge said, "You're a bit of a beast when your temper gets going, young Jimi Jack.

Maybe we can put some of this rage to good use down there in the camp".

I was not sure what the Sarge meant but I was certain he had some sort of a plan brewing.

At about 2.30am the Sarge and I entered the club house of the camp.

Drones flew over us every few minutes and only a couple of Sad Sun bandits patrolled the main paths of the camp.

The clubhouse smelled musty and the walls were filled with antique hunting weapons of all sorts.

Bows and arrows, swords, spears, axes, poison arrows, Blowpipes, and even a couple of stuffed animal heads, but what caught my eye were a set of Boomerangs.

They were things of beauty - throwing wings which returned to the thrower, which could be deadly when used properly.

They were an aerodynamic marvel, a weapon which flew and returned to you and we all know how much my family loved airplanes and flight.

Creeping in the shadows.

I helped myself to two boomerangs off the wall and heard the Sarge say quietly into the headphone of my helmet.

"A good choice, Jimi Jack.

You are a Beast and now you are armed with a couple of hunting Boomerangs - You are the Boomerang Beast".

So that was the moment my nickname was born and I was not to know it then, but later that night, I was truly going to earn that name.

The Sarge planned to immobilize the Sad Sun drones by destroying the control centre which was located somewhere in the camp.

He already had explosives with him, which he collected from the trailer of his vehicle but we did not know where the control centre was and also how heavily it was guarded by the Sad Sun soldiers.

Together, we crept along, hiding in the shadows of the log-built dormitory and kitchen huts until we saw what looked like a building of importance.

It was busy with Sad Sun soldiers coming and going in and out of the entrance.

Drones also buzzed overhead more frequently than elsewhere so we guessed this must be the control centre.

"You stay here, Jimi Jack.

I'm going in to take a closer look", the Sarge said to me.

I nodded and off he went, all the while soldiers passed by without a word being spoken and drones flew overhead.

One drone hovered right above my head and I thought it had seen me with an infra-red camera but it moved away slowly.

I thought maybe Lewis's soldier suit was eliminating my body heat so I could not be seen by the drones.

I waited motionless for, what seemed an eternity for the Sarge to return, but the Sarge did not come back.

Then I heard three-gun shots in quick succession so I decided that I had to make my way into the building.

The corridor lights were very dim and a distant hum could be heard from the room at the end.

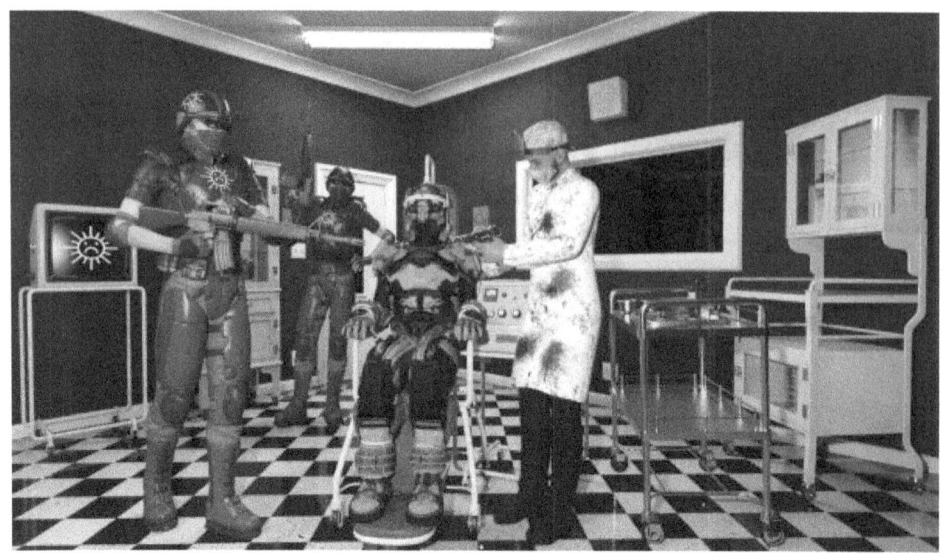

The Sarge strapped down.

As I peeked in to the room, I could see two Sad Sun soldiers had the Sarge strapped on to a medical restraining chair and it looked like he had been shot in both legs and his right shoulder.

That would have been the three shots I heard earlier.

The Sarge was moaning and another person walked back and forth wearing a white lab coat stained with blood and he was doing something to the Sarge.

I leaped in to the room and threw both boomerangs one after the other, at each solder's head, picked up one of their rifles and smashed an injector instrument out of the doctor's hands.

One of the Sad Sun soldiers was getting up off the floor and suddenly he lunged at me with a large hunting knife which I avoided by stepping back quickly.

I picked up the large boomerang and used it to keep my attacker at a distance.

The opportunity arose where I used the boomerang like an axe and struck the soldier in his eye whereupon he went down on his knees groaning.

I ripped the wrist straps off the Sarge and released his ankle straps also, but the doctor was heading for the exit.

I aimed, and then hurled the large boomerang towards him where it struck the doctor on the back of his head knocking him clean out.

By now the Sarge was up and armed with a rifle he collected from the floor and without hesitation the Sarge walked over and mercilessly, shot the two soldiers dead and then also the doctor.

The Sarge said, "This way Jimi Jack", heading for a door, limping badly, bleeding, and moaning in pain.

Inside, was a cold, darkened room full of rack after rack of computer equipment to which the Sarge attached several magnetic explosive devices.

"OK", let's get out of here", he said heading for the outside exit.

I picked up my boomerangs and walked closely behind the Sarge, out of the building, into the trees and back up the steep hill.

Towards the Lookout hut.

"BOOM, BOOM, BOOM", was what we heard coming from the building we had just left.

Flames engulfed the log building, shattered the glass and drones dropped out of the sky.

We felt the shockwave through the ground and even through our boots, as we made our way further up the mountain.

We kept climbing the hill until we could see the whole camp below once again.

We could see Sad Sun soldiers scurrying about like black ants, climbing into vehicles and going this way and that but not a single drone was in the air.

I was just thinking that the Sarge had done what he set out to do when suddenly he collapsed in front of me.

"What's wrong, Sarge", I said feeling concerned for my new friend.

"They've killed me", he said.

"They shot me three times but also injected radioactive poison into my stomach.

You did well to rescue me, Boomerang Beast.

Shame you didn't come ten minutes earlier".

I was heartbroken to hear the Sarge say that.

"...but you said to stay there...", I answered, feeling really guilty.

"I'm only joking, Jimi Jack.

You did really well to rescue me or I would be dead already."

He paused and then said, "I would be proud to have had you in my squad.

Now you just have to survive this new worlds' craziness.

Get away from here and go North - find people - find your family..."

The Sarge stopped breathing.

The Sarge coughed blood each time he spoke and his last words rang around in my mind over and over.

"Find your Family, Find your Family".

I did not know it then, but at that very moment my Family was out searching for me in the Family Flyer.

At the top of the hill was a small wooden Park Rangers, lookout hut, where we took refuge and rested.

I stayed with the Sarge all night cradling his head on my lap while the temperature dropped outside and the commotion in the camp stopped.

It was a cold grey dawn while a large bright moon glowed through gaps in the cloud and the snow fell around us until the Sarge stopped breathing.

The next few days I headed North as the Sarge suggested, walking mainly by night, avoiding all vehicles and Sad Sun soldiers in vehicles.

I hunted duck with the boomerangs, I fished in streams and ate it raw avoiding making fires.

I collected berries but noticed the pink mist was more prevalent day by day.

Birds had become silent, bees had stopped buzzing, rabbits were dead on the paths that I walked and I could not risk drinking any water, so I figured I had better not fend off the land any more.

I walked and walked for days until I was so hungry, dehydrated and exhausted that I collapsed, falling down a hill, unconscious.

I awoke to several blurry young faces staring down at me and trying to prise the helmet from my head to pour water into my mouth.

I had found a tribe of young people - or should I say, that they had found me.

They nursed me back to health over the next few weeks and as I was the oldest, I became their leader.

The boys even continued to call me "The Boomerang Beast" and I stayed with them for many months until Mum, Dad and Skye found me in the Family Flyer.

Having recounted my story, I was so happy to be laying on my bed in my room, back home, at Freedom Point.

The invaders on the lookout.

Chapter 09 - Invaders.

After a quick check around the house, turning the boiler on for hot water and making sure the girls were alright, I switched on the security, video recording system which showed, on a monitor, anything that had happened over the last few months.

I sped through the days and weeks until I came to the section where the two Landover vehicles and a group of people had arrived, and were trying to break in.

There were two men, a young boy and the lady with her head covered with a hoodie, carrying a small child.

They tried bashing on the concrete shields with bricks and gesturing and shouting at the cameras to let them in.

They tried levering the concrete doors with logs and other tools until they finally gave up and made their campsite in our carpark where they lit a bonfire.

I was thrilled that our security system was robust enough to withstand these invaders.

The next day they tried the concrete doors all over again, only this time the young boy spray painted the luminant green Sad Sun logo on our lookout gantry wall.

Two uncared-for vehicles were still at the base of the mountain in the main carpark but there was no sign of any of the invaders.

They had obviously seen and heard us fly over them, land, and were probably hiding somewhere nearby.

I was happy that we were sealed in, safe and sound in our house, but I was ready just in case they started trouble.

I switched to the live cameras monitoring the small runway and found all of the invaders around the Family Flyer.

One of the two men, the older man, with straggly blond hair, was hammering and trying to prise open the cockpit stair door of the Family Flyer with a crowbar, while he precariously perched on a makeshift wooden ladder.

The young boy appeared to be assisting him, holding on to the ladder.

The lady carrying the child was on lookout and the second man with dark hair was crouched down low, on guard, looking all around.

A formidable bunch.

I decided to remotely start up the Flyer engines, giving the invaders a fright and made them run for cover.

Then I remotely piloted it up and around, to bring the aircraft into the hangar on the restaurant and attraction level, just below.

It was effortless, except I did not know at the time that the young boy had foolishly, or was it bravely, hitched a ride on the Family Flyer, holding onto one of the landing gear wheels.

I had no idea that when I brought and landed the aeroplane into the hangar, I was also bringing in an unwanted passenger into our property.

The invaders grouped together on the landing pad, talking quietly amongst themselves.
I did not know it then, but at first, they discussed that we had flown the aircraft into the hangar and wondered what we were going to do next, and then they were giving each other high fives.

I guess that was when they realised the young boy was inside the hanger.

When the Family Flyer engines stopped, the young boy, whose name was Dan, gingerly stepped on to the hangar floor.

He was lucky he did not fall off the aircraft to his death onto the rocks, hundreds of feet below.

He stayed close to the Family Flyer to start with, before ducking behind drums of oil, furniture and other equipment in the hanger.

He carefully avoided the cameras panning from side to side, spotted a fire escape exit door and pushed quietly against the bar to open it, letting the rest of his group in.

The alarm on the door triggered a silent flashing warning sign on the security screen and showed that the invaders had entered the property but no one was there to see it. Kat was busy preparing a meal in the kitchen, while Skye was in her room resting and Jimi Jack and I were now in the living room, chatting and having a cup of tea.

The two uninvited men were now armed with a hammer and a large wrench, respectively, and the woman carrying the small child, carried an axe, while Dan, the young boy, made do with a short length of chain.

They looked a formidable bunch, and very scary, walking purposefully, through the hanger, towards the emergency exit stairwell.

The intruders attack.

Jimi Jack took a large sip of tea, and mid-slurp, stopped abruptly, with eyes wide, and stared at a point just behind me.

"What's wrong?" I said, "Dad, behind you - the visitors," Jimi Jack said, with tension in his voice.

I stood up quickly and turned around to face the intruders, to be met with a hammer blow to my head.

"Dad!" was the last thing I heard as my vision went black, and I fell to the floor.

Jimi Jack reacted like lightning, punching the man with the hammer square on the jaw. The man was out cold and went down, fast.

Before the second man had time to react, Jimi Jack had his arm twisted behind his back and with his free hand, bashed this man's head on to the tiled floor of the living room with a thump, knocking him out too.

Hearing the commotion from elsewhere, Kat and Skye came running in to the battle going on in the living room.

The woman, with child in her arms, raised her axe near Kat's face and Kat said, "Really? You have both your men down."

The young boy, Dan, leaped onto Skye's back from behind, bringing her down to the ground and began to strangle her with his length of chain—but in one quick turn, Skye had Dan on his stomach, with his face pushed into the living room rug.

This just left Kathleen facing the woman with the axe in hand, both staring intensely into each other's eyes when the baby in the woman's arms, started to cry.

Kat held up her hands, open palms facing the woman in a gesture of peace, and said, "Come on, let's stop this before someone really gets hurt."

I said from the floor, rubbing my head and trying to stand up, "Somebody is already hurt - me."

Tea party.

Kat spoke in a gentle voice to the woman.

"Give me the axe - please.

Let's get some milk for the baby.

Come on, let's all sit down and have some tea and cake."

Dan, who had now been released by Skye, sat up and nodded enthusiastically from the floor and said, "Cake.

I like cake. Mmmmm".

The woman handed over the axe to Kat and Jimi Jack relieved the two men of their weapons.

I went over, a little unsteadily on my feet, to revive the older man knocked down by Jimi Jack's punch.

His eyes were now starting to open and he was mumbling something, his hair untidy and a dribble of blood stained, saliva oozing from the side of his mouth.

"It's okay, Henrik," the woman said, going down to the floor to look after the man.

"They're being friendly.

They've just offered us tea and cake and milk for the baby."

"Sounds like a plan," I said, pointing to the dining table just metres away and rubbing my head, "This way."

I first headed for the kitchen freezer looking for some ice to pack in a cloth to use against my throbbing head.

It wasn't long before we found out that the two men were called Henrik, who was the older one with the hammer, and Max who was the younger man with the large wrench.

The woman's name was Bella and the baby was called Freddie.

Dan apologised for attacking Skye with the chain, and as we all settled around the dining table the girls brought out a marvellous selection of cakes to go with our tea.

Henrik said to me, "Sorry, mate, l didn't mean..."

"It's okay," I said, holding the ice pack against my right temple. "Where are you folks headed?"

I wondered what the visitors were planning.

Were they thinking of staying indefinitely?

Would they try taking over our house by force again or even try stealing the Family Flyer?

Shocking the intruders.

All I knew for sure was that it was too risky to have our new "friends" in the house for any longer than we had to.

We made them comfortable for the night by putting a camp bed in with Skye, and Dan slept in her room while the two men slept on the sofas in the living room and Bella and the baby stayed in our guest room.

I wasn't going to take any further chances, so Kat and I said goodnight to everyone, and I set a video alarm monitor up in our bedroom.

If anyone moved, I would know about it.

Before long I saw Skye and Dan raid the kitchen for cookies and milk laughing about something.

Bella paced up and down the guest room with little Freddie over one Shoulder trying to get him to sleep but the two men, Henrik and Max, were suspiciously, nowhere to be seen.

"Now, what", I said quietly to Kat.

I flicked through the cameras monitoring the living room, the corridors outside the bedrooms and bathrooms, and then I found them back in the hangar with the Family Flyer.

Once again, they were trying to open the cockpit stair door.

The communication ear-piece, by the side of the bed, was flashing, so I put it on.

"Dad, are you watching this?" Jimi Jack whispered into my earpiece who was also watching a duplicate security monitor in his room.

"Yes, I can see them.

Don't worry, I've got a couple of surprises for them."

First, I let them try pulling on the edges of the door for a short while.

I opened a screen on the iPad entitled, "Flyer Safety Measures", and clicked on, "Arm Doors".

The label changed from green to red.

The two men pulled again on the edges of the door with all their might, only this time, one hundred and twenty volts shot through their fingers and bodies, raising the hair on their heads and catapulted both of them backwards through the air, making them land several meters away from the Family Flyer.

The intruders leaving.

"Whoa," I heard Jimi Jack say, in my earpiece.

"Are they going to be okay?"

"There're fine.

They just had a bit of a shock," I said.

"But, I'm going to end their silliness once and for all."

"No, Dad, don't kill them," Jimi Jack pleaded.

"Of course not," I reassured my son.

"But, these two will have a headache in the morning."

I pressed another button on the airplane's "Safety Measures", page and this time an almost inaudible hissing sound began just below, and outside the Family Flyers', Staircase door.

A few more seconds later and Henrik and Max were out cold - unconscious, on the hangar floor.

I went to bed much happier, knowing that I had just initiated the, "Activate sleeping gas", button.

It looked like we were all finally going to get a good night's sleep.

The next morning, we dressed for action as we wanted to start training again with the airplane, do some sky diving, add some modifications to the Family Flyer, so escorted our guests to their Landcover's, downstairs.

We gave them food, water and fuel but I felt uncomfortable about asking Bella, Dan and little Freddie, to leave, but I was sure that if it came to it, Bella's loyalties would lie with the others, and I was also sure it was a really bad idea that Dan was going off with Henrik and Max really did not look like good role models for a young teenage boy.

I was not surprised to see Dan give Skye a big hug after which she said, "Take care, mate".

"Yeah, you too", he replied, with a slight tremble of uncertainty and sadness, in his voice.

We watched the two Landrover vehicles start up and then drive out of the main visitor's carpark for some minutes and we all waved until they disappeared into the distance, leaving nothing but a hazy dust trail, and a thick, uneasy silence, but then…

Up the emergency stairwell.

We heard and felt, "BOOM" followed by another "BOOM", from every level of our mountain.

Flames and thick black smoke began pouring out of every window, door, air vent and crack, at Freedom Point and our home.

The shock waves were so intense that the whole mountain shook, knocking us all off our feet, onto the ground.

I could only think that our visitors felt very upset about the electric shock and sleeping gas and that we were sending them away, and rather than allow us a comfortable life in our lovely home, they chose to sabotage it, destroy what we had created and leave us with nothing.

They must have had the explosives in their trucks, which they attached to the many tanks of fuel in the hangers on all the different levels, which they detonated using a timer, or maybe even by remote control from their trucks, as they drove away.

Luckily, none of us waited in the house to say goodbye to our guests or we would surely have been injured or even, killed by the explosions.

I could now only think of our beloved Family Flyer, which was sitting in a hangar on the middle level, which was now probably destroyed in the explosion and blaze.

I did not waste a second in pulling my iPhone from my belt holster.

I took a chance and hoped the engines would start, so I could ram the hangar door open because the doors would not slide open on their own when I pressed the, "Open Hanger Door" button.

From where we stood on the lower carpark level, it looked hopeless, with the hangar door on fire on the inside but I was not going to give up hope on the Family Flyer.

Kat and Skye were in shock, and both girls faces looked really upset.

Even Jimi Jack was speechless but before I could say a word, he sprinted off up the emergency stairwell at the side of the mountain.

"Jimi Jack - wait", I shouted at him but he just kept going.

Freedom Point on fire.

Kat screamed, "No, no, Jimi, come back - it's too dangerous", but the Boomerang Beast took no notice.

Even the dried grass and bushes around us were on fire, and we could feel the searing heat from several meters away.

I called out, "Everybody, move further away from the mountain and get behind some cover.

I'm going to try to ram the hangar door from the inside with the Family Flyer."

Using the iPhone to control the aircraft in the hanger, on the middle level above us, I managed to start the engines, tilt them forwards and hoped the aeroplane was going to respond to my commands.

Seconds later, and hovering at one metre, it rammed the inside of the hanger doors with a huge bang but the doors were just too strong to break down.

Meanwhile, after racing up the emergency stairwell, Jimi Jack had entered the burning hanger with the Family Flyer hovering just off the ground, kicking up smoke, flames and dust, while I tried crashing into the sliding doors once again.

Luckily, 3J's was in his Boomerang Beast protective suit and leaped into the flames at the back of the hanger, when suddenly, a large air conditioning unit and the connected ducting, collapsed onto him, knocking him unconscious and pinning his body and legs down.

Fire and smoke raged all around 3J's and it looked hopeless.

Below, in the carpark, Kat, Skye and I had moved well away from the many, jet fuel induced, fires, raging all around us.

"Where was 3J's?

Is he OK? What should I do", I thought.

I already lost him once.

Should I go after him?

I tried to get to the emergency stairwell but could not get very far through the smoke and flames.

BB rescued by Kat and Skye.

Jimi Jack was now waking up in the hanger, his armoured suit and helmet giving him some protection from the heat and smoke but he still could not get to the hanger door controls, which were several metres across the other side of the hanger, through the flames and smoke, and he was still trapped under the air conditioning unit and ducting.

Much to my concern, Kat and Skye ran off together in the opposite direction of the stairs, towards the large yellow, tower crane, with Kat screaming, "I've got an idea".

I covered myself with a builder's blue tarpaulin I found in the carpark and headed back up the flaming stairwell.
I managed to get to the hanger level, with the Family Flyer and our son, but the doors were still jammed shut, on fire, and I was locked out.

The Boomerang Beast was now semi-conscious and lifted his large boomerang above his head.

He aimed for a moment at the door control buttons several metres away, and let the boomerang fly.

The boomerang whistled through the air as it spun, gracefully cutting through the smoke and fire in the hanger causing mini vortexes at its tips, until it connected perfectly with the green, "Open Hanger Doors", button.

The hanger doors creaked and groaned for a moment and opened about half way, before they finally jammed once again, due to the heat.

Then the motor whined, sparks pouring from it, and finally exploded with a large and quite unimpressive, white puff of smoke.

Some roof panels had come away in the ceiling above Jimi Jack and a moment later Skye was hitching a ride on the giant crane hook, dropping down rapidly to where Jimi Jack was trapped.

Kat, now operating the crane by a cable remote, while balancing high above on a roof beam, had smashed through the roof of the hanger lowering Skye, riding the hook, down to rescue Jimi Jack.

I entered the hanger fully aware as to what was going on and the danger each of us was in. Once on the floor by 3J's, Skye attached the crane hook to the air conditioning unit and Kat, using the crane's remote, lifted the air conditioning unit up a few inches off 3J's, just enough for Skye to pull the Boomerang Beast out.

The Family Flyer bursts through the hanger doors.

Seconds later, Kat was also with us, having climbed down a roof ladder to the hanger floor.

All four of us hurriedly clambered up the stair door of the airplane and took our positions in the cockpit.

Skye and I dived into our respective seats while Jimi Jack removed his helmet and Kat closed the stair door.

"Smash the doors down", I said to Skye.

"Are you sure", she asked.

I simply nodded.

Still hovering at one metre, Skye set the power to full forward thrust and as the airplane's jets moved the aircraft towards the doors, we witnessed the most beautiful thing we had all seen in a very long time.

The Family Flyer burst through the burning hangar doors, which were now partially opened due to 3J's efforts, disintegrating the doors, as the airplane passed through the flames, metal, and burning wood.

The aeroplane looked so beautiful as it sliced through the flaming hanger doors reminding me of a whale breaking through the surface of the ocean.

It was just a home built aircraft, but it was our aeroplane and also our lifeline, our pride and joy and part of our family.

We did not know it at that precise moment, but it was going to be our crutch to lean on from now on, it would be our travelling home - the only home we had left, and was soon going to take us on to our next adventure.

The Family Flyer signified the unity of our family, our freedom and the hope for our future.

THE END

Music Album Title: Family Flyer 01. By Jack Ezra.

Song Title - Run Times - Who might sing it.

1) We're Family. 04.11. THE FAMILY.
2) Wake Up. 03.37. JACK & BANSHEE.
3) Road Trip. 03.21. 3J'S.
4) How Do I Decide. 02.22. 3J'S.
5) I Just Want To Fly. 03.28. SKYE.
6) Unconditional. 02.55. KAT.
7) All Around Me. 03.32. MATI.
8) It's Just A Dream. 03.53. 3J'S.
9) Dance Your Troubles Away. 03.22. KAT.
10) Christmas Moon. 05.56. THE SARGE.
11) The Boomerang Beast. 03.10. 3J'S.
12) I Don't Wanna Fight. 03.20. 3J'S.
13) Dangerous Drones. 03.07. JACK.
14) Simply Just a Man. 04.16. JACK.
15) Freedom Point. 03.44. 3J'S.

The band in this book is called the BeXt and is a fictional band created by Author/ Singer/ Song-writer, Jack Ezra.

The band consists of…

Jack Johnson - Guitar/ Vocals

Kathleen Johnson - Keyboards/ Vocals

Skye Jett Johnson - Drums/ Vocals

Jimi Jack Johnson - Bass/ Vocals.

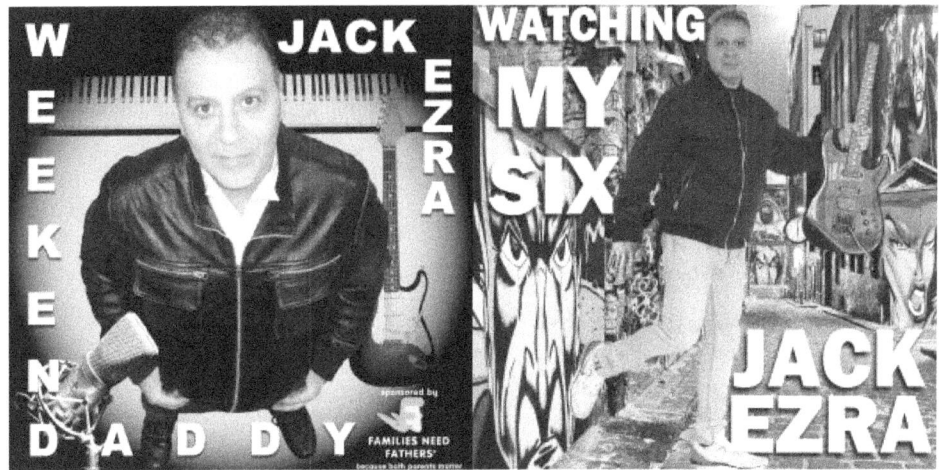

Other Music Albums by Jack Ezra.
Weekend Daddy - Watching My Six
Premonition Remastered - Unidentified

Note:
While the band may be from the author's imagination, the songs and music are certainly NOT imaginary and can be downloaded to accompany the story of the Family Flyer and the Boomerang Beast.

If this book were a movie or a stage show then these songs would be playing throughout.

An idea of who might sing the song is indicated after the song title and time.

Wake up

Wake up Wake up Wake up Wake up
Wake up
To the devastation
Wake up
To the situation
Wake up, wake up, wake up

I saw a child taking centre stage
at the United Nations
We thank you Greta for your inspiration
On climate change and deforestation

It time to act
it's not time to cry
The talking talking talking's wasting time
Our World's a jewel
Gold white green and blue
It spins in sadness
Remember it's your home too

Wake up
To the devastation
Wake up
To the situation
Wake up, wake up, wake up

The child said
there's a change coming
You have the choice
Don't be part of the problem
Come on take part
Join the green revolution
And instead you can be
Part of the solution

Dangerous Drones

No love no feelings
No soul just cold programming
Their engines turn
Bright lights they burn
Their guns shoot fire
We can run or expire

And they're so Dangerous
Dangerous Drones

Their dark steel flys
Cameras for eyes
They made them smart
Without a heart
They're gonna get you
Shoot you down
No hesitation - annihilation

And they're so Dangerous
Dangerous Drones

Roadtrip

Roadtrip Roadtrip
Me and my friends
Having fun together
Roadtrip Roadtrip Roadtrip

We're going on a road trip
Won't you come along
I just love that sweet sensation
Rolling all day long
I don't know the destination
But I don't mind

So if you want to go
Sit back and enjoy the show
'Caus you don't need
A reason to ride

We're going on a road trip
For a week or more
Get to relax
Listen to music
Play some sports and go for walks
Starting to sense that we could be in danger
But I'm not sure

I Don't Wanna fight

I don't wanna fight

Maybe we can talk a truce with each other
Find a kind of peace

Let's not try to be
Mad at you or me
Over and over
I'm sure we can work it out

If our world
Could live in harmony
What a place it would be

I don't wanna fight

Life is too short
There's not time enough
To do what we want
How do we make sure
We spend time with the ones
The ones that we love

I don't wanna fight

Maybe we could show some love for each other
Don't want to make you cry

Unconditional

It's unconditional
A mother's love
It's unbelievable
Just how it is

Shout it out and celebrate it

Parents and children
Know that it's real

Shout it out and celebrate it

Special to Mother's
And nothing can break
Natures connection
Of pleasure and pain

Shout it out and celebrate it

Unconditional

Christmas Moon

Christmas Moon
I'm just a soldier boy
One of ten thousand down
I'm shot three times and sure
My friends have all died through war

Will I be here tomorrow
Will I meet my doom
I'm gazing up at heaven
Will I be there soon
Christmas Moon
You're so blue

I know that I
Will never see my love again
I will miss those hugs and kisses
My soul will fly as I will die
At last I will be free
Christmas Moon

Home seems so far away
I gaze up to see
What is waiting there for me
No life to live no love to give
No future plans for me
Christmas Moon
You're so blue

Being kissed by flakes of snow which drift like dreams today
Like your sweet lips they peck my cheek exactly where I lay
My cold and bloody muddy end may come this afternoon
I might pass and so might you - stands Sentinel the moon
Christmas Moon
You're so blue

It's Just A Dream

I woke up puzzled by my dream
Kneeling on one knee
Asking my love to marry me
Viewed on a big screen

A flight of fancy
Which could mean something
Not to be taken too seriously
It's just a dream
It's just a dream

A grey alien handed me
A sparkling diamond ring
His space ship hovering
For all humanity to see

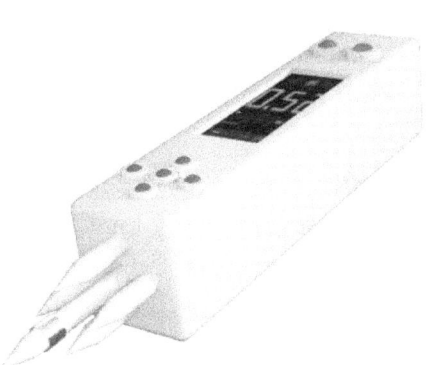

Some people believe
There's a mystery in sleep
Are you one of them now
Are you one of them now

Are you of the mind
That says our dreams
Transcends space and time
Are you one of them now
Are you one of them now
And all dreams mean something
To someone
Stop it

An empty stadium jam packed full
Of singing people
My Girlfriends face turned into my sisters
That was so disturbing

A flight of fancy
Which could mean something
Not to be taken too seriously
It's just a dream
It's just a dream

Dance Your Troubles Away

Always moving
From place to place
I can hardly
Remember his face

And when you're lonely
I can recommend something that you can do

Dance dance dance dance
Dance your troubles away
Dance dance dance dance
Dance your troubles away

I can confirm that
My life's a sadder space
To lose my baby
Gone without a trace

And when you're lonely
I can recommend something that you can do

Dance dance dance dance
Dance your troubles away
Dance dance dance dance
Dance your troubles away

Hear me now
Can't seem to sleep much
The stress is too great
Our World's in turmoil
But this might just lift that weight
Oh yeah

And when you're lonely
I can recommend something that you can do

Dance dance dance dance
Dance your troubles away
Dance dance dance dance
Dance your troubles away

How Do I Decide

I've been unloved for so long
And just when I felt I belong

How do I - How do I decide

Just when I felt love for someone
How can I forget it and move along

How do I - How do I decide
Won't you tell me now

Between a rock and a hard place
A happy or sad face
A dark or a bright day
Do I Leave or do I stay
Face forwards or turn away
Rain check for another day

Won't you tell me now
How do I - How do I
How do I decide- How do I decide
How do I - How do I
How do I decide- How do I decide

All Around Me

You make me feel - safer and secure
And that's what having friends are for

And when you blow me a kiss
I already miss yer
Or give me a hug
'Caus you are my bestie
And when I'm feeling like this
We're always together
I know for sure

I can feel the love
All around me

You give me strength and always
so much more
And that's what having friends are for

And when you blow me a kiss
I already miss yer
Or give me a hug
'Caus you are my bestie
And when I'm feeling like this
We're always together
I know for sure

I can feel the love
All around me

You can
Count on me - for ever more
And that's what having friends are for

I Just Want To Fly

Walking - is just not for me
And driving fast - might set you free
Be cooler - manoeuvre
A jet in the clouds with me
And sooner - or later
I know that you'll agree

I just want to fly
I just want to fly

Glide around in a metal bird
I know how that sounds just a tad up-surd
You can be the pilot and take control
You can grab the stick and up and down we'll go
It's like a drug—the blue sky
I Need my fix and I'm gona get high

I just want to fly
I just want to fly

There's nothing you - can compare to flight
Just come with me
We'll touch the stars tonight

And when your down or feeling low
I know the place you need to go
Leave the ground - give it a try
Spread your wings and you will fly

I just want to fly
I just want to fly

Simply Just A Man

They say I'm rock solid reliability
And in some ways I hope that's true
The very height of sensibility
But it's a lot to live up to

The expectations are so far from reality
I can only be just who I am

So please forgive me
If I'm simply just a man
No superhero
'Cause I'm simply just a man

Furthermore I'm just a guy in love
A Father does his best to guide his children
And if they ever hurt the ones I love
I couldn't help what I might do

The expectations are so far from reality
I can only be just who I am

So please forgive me
If I'm simply just a man
No superhero
'Cause I'm simply just a man

**Sincere thanks to
Tracy Collins
for her
additional vocals on this song.**

You're more than simply just a man to me
And to the Family you're Daddy too
You're the person that we love more and more each day
So don't put yourself down
In this silly way

The expectations are so far from reality
I can only be just who I am

So please forgive me
If I'm simply just a man
No superhero

We're Family

Mama rose - to fame and fortune
On the catwalk - she was a superstar
Daddy worked - hard as a teacher
Before he married Mama
Always knew they'd go far

We're a family
We're family

Skye and Jimi-had the best
Mother and Father - they could ever wish for
But round the corner - there lurked disaster
Death and destruction
Was knocking on their door

We're a family
We're family

I love my family
Take it up

Trying to stay alive - through the smoke and fire
The Family spirit - love of adventure
Kept us together - with that one desire
From out of nothing - they built the Flyer

The Boomerang Beast

Hey yeah
Please forgive me
Cause I can't stand up here
And watch this silly fighting any longer
And I can bet cha
If your willing
We can reach a good solution
By the morning

Just listen to me
I am the boomerang beast
Huh boomerang
He is the boomerang beast
Huh boomerang

There's nothing gained - from waring
It's such a shame
That we can't trust
And we can't love any more

Just listen to me
I am the boomerang beast
Huh boomerang
He is the boomerang beast
Huh boomerang

I wanna give you something
To throw at yer
I wanna give you something
To hold on to

You can live this life
In hopelessness
Or you can fly free like a boomerang
Just listen to me

It's circling around
Don't let me down

Freedom Point

Home is what my heart aches for
I feel I should say
'Caus my life's in so many pieces
And my Family seems so far away

Who—will save me now
I'm just missing you
Missing you—Missing You

Freedom Point
Freedom Point
Freedom Point
That's my home

I need some stability
And some rationality
I've seen my friends mowed down
Their blood stains the ground
I'm looking for some kind of sanity

Who—will save me now
I'm just missing you
Missing you—Missing You

Freedom Point
Freedom Point
Freedom Point
That's my home

I lay my head down under an uncertain sky
But when will I see loneliness
Turn to joy

Who—will save me now
I'm just missing you
Missing you—Missing You

Freedom Point

This Music Album download sites.

iTunes

YouTube Content ID

TikTok

Amazon Music

Music Unlimited

Boomplay Music

Spotify

Amazon Prime Music

United Media Agency

Apple Music

Rdio

Saavn

Google Play

Napster

Muve

YouTube Music

iTunes Match

Music Island

I Heart Radio

Facebook

Tencent

Netease Cloud Music

Tidal

Yandex

Deezer

Instagram

Zvooq

Resso

Simfy Africa

Trebel

Pandora

Snapchat

Joox

Amazon

Audible Magic

Anghami Music

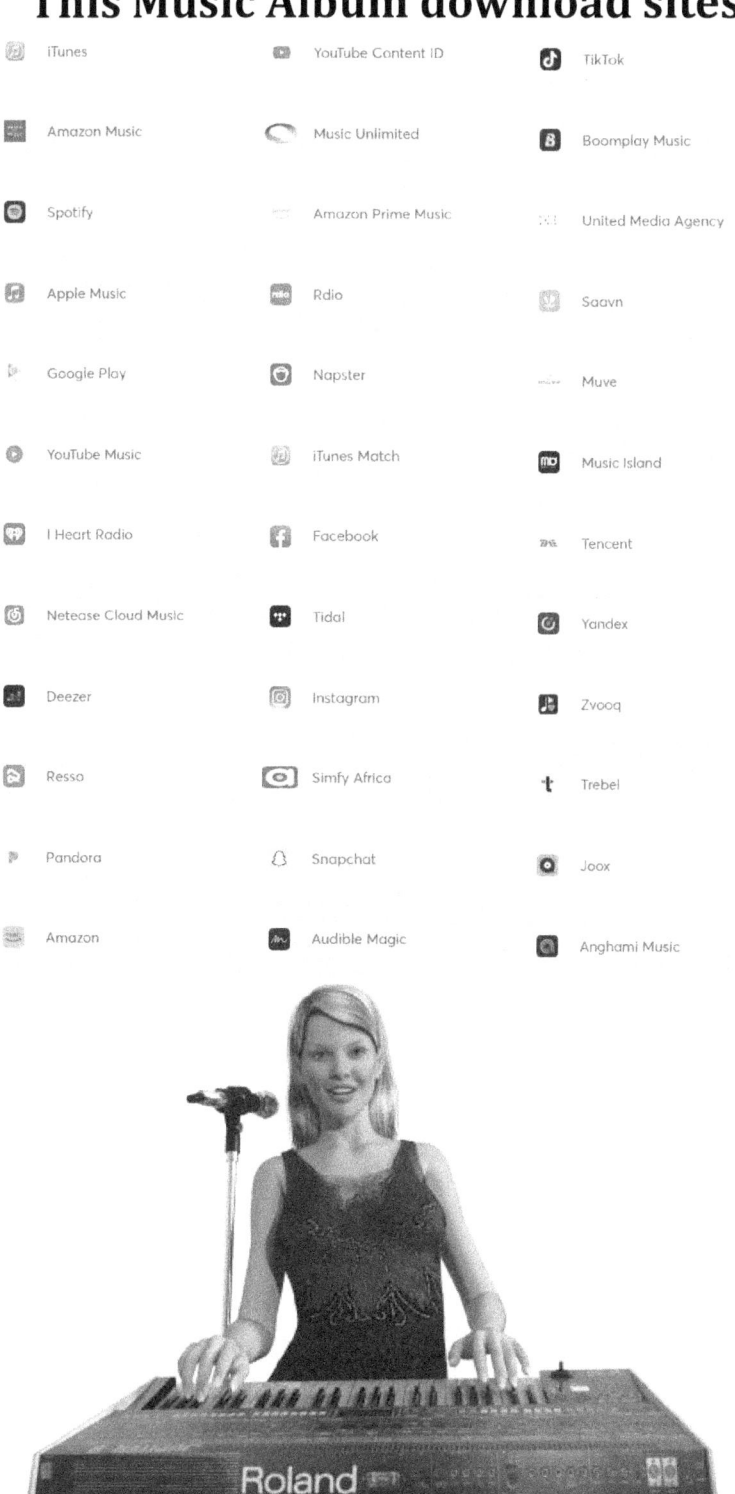

www.ingramcontent.com/pod-product-compliance
Lightning Source LLC
Chambersburg PA
CBHW050402030726
47503CB00006B/1978